THE SHORT LIFE

DENNIS JERNIGAN

All songs (words and music) written by Dennis Jernigan unless otherwise noted.

Edited by www.darrenthornberry.com | Cover design by www.angelahaddon.com

Published by Dennis Jernigan/Shepherd's Heart Music, Inc. | 7804 West Fern Mountain, Muskogee, OK 74401 | www.dennisjernigan.com

Jernigan, Dennis: The Short Life

Paperback ISBN: 978-1-948772-09-9

Large Print ISBN: 978-1-948772-11-2

ePub ISBN: 978-1-948772-22-8

1

FIRST CLASS

> Waiting, waiting, waiting. All my life, I've been waiting for my life to begin, as if somehow my life was ahead of me, and that someday I would arrive at it.
>
> CAMRYN MANHEIM

Jake Owens had lived several troubled lifetimes in his 30 years. To say he had overcome many struggles would be a laughable understatement. After all he had been through, people who knew him best considered him a hero. But even as Jake boarded the plane, he still fought those feelings from childhood—that he was a loser. Although he had gone through hell and lived to tell about it, the demons he still faced would frighten and discourage anyone who could see the reality in his head.

Yet, everything he imagined as a child to be out of reach was now coming true in his adult life. He never thought having a woman to love him would be possible, that marriage could be a beautiful thing if one put the work into it that real relationships require. He never thought it possible to be a great dad to his son and daughter, simply because of the lousy example his own father had been. He never dreamed that holding down a good-paying job could be a reality. Calling the home he grew up in "unstable" would be very charitable.

But here he was. Married for five wonderful years to his high school sweetheart, Olivia. Livy, as he called her, had been there to help him pick up the shards of his life during that terrible senior year of high school. She was the one who taught him how to value a woman as an equal, helping him understand the subtleties of relationship. Real, life-inducing, life-altering, life-changing relationship. She had waded into the mess of his life and walked out of it with him, even when he felt his life had not been worth saving.

And the kids. He had dreamed of one day being a dad, purposing in his heart that he would never be the kind of dad his own father had been—or not been—to him. His heart and mind were easily overwhelmed with love whenever he thought of his children. To him, they were worth dying for—a notion he knew had never crossed his own dad's mind. Loving his kids was one of the greatest joys of his life. Showering them with gifts early on, he came to realize (thanks to Livy's gentle admonishment) that his children needed balance in their life more than they needed gifts. She helped him see that consistency from a dad who was "there" was more important than any temporary gift. He wanted his children to see and know how significant they were to him.

Even the names he and Livy had given their children were deeply significant. Brock, for their firstborn, now two years old, means "badger," and badgers are diligent, focused and passionate creatures, willing to fight to the death. He wanted his son to know that he would fight to the death for him...that every time he heard his name, he would be reminded that he was worth fighting for. This concept was foreign to Jake in his formative years.

And then there was his baby girl. Only four weeks old, he and Livy had talked for weeks about what to name her. They had agreed on the meaning of her name before they actually gave her a name! Since he had grown up feeling hopeless, Jake had asked Livy to consider a name that reflected hopefulness. Nadia is the name they chose in the hope that she would always be reminded of a truth Jake had only learned as an adult: As long as he was breathing, there was hope! Even as much as he believed it for his children—that they were worth fighting for and that as long as they were breathing there was hope—he found such hopefulness almost too good to be true in his own life. But the more he'd thought about it as truth, the more his feelings of dread had subsided through the years.

It was on days like today, when good things happened, that he found his inner battles the most difficult. After college, he landed the dream job of dream jobs. A creative design major, he had envisioned one day working as a creative director for a major ad agency. Now his day had come. A friend had turned him on to a job posted on the website of one of the major agencies in Texas. Nexus Texas was a leader in all things creative in the marketing world in the Ft. Worth/Dallas Metroplex. Known for cutting edge visuals and envelope-pushing creative designs, to get a foot in the door there was next to impossible.

When his friend encouraged him to at least fill out the application, he had, as usual, heard the voice of his father echoing through all the years. "Are you kidding me? Why would they even look at the application of someone like you? What would a place like that want with a peckerwood like you?"

Those words clashed with what Livy constantly spoke into him—that his father's past words had no power over his present reality unless he let them. This had caused Jake quite the battle. But, as he was growing more accustomed to doing, he put off those thoughts and replaced them with the truth of who he had come to believe he was now. Completing the application, he giggled to himself as he clicked the "Submit" button, the simple act of filling out the form a major victory in his mind over those echoes from the past.

As he was directed to his seat in first class, something he still found unbelievable and quite exciting, he recounted the day's events. His supervisor had given him the much-sought-after task of representing Nexus Texas at the National Marketing Convention in Las Vegas. Since Livy had just given birth, he would be making the trip alone. He had rehearsed his presentation over and over again to the point that Livy finally said amidst laughter, "Jacob Matthew Owens, you could give this presentation in your sleep! Enough already! Give it a rest! You'll slay them!" Having come to cherish such outbursts from his always-encouraging Livy, Jake had rested well the night before.

Since his flight was so early this morning, he carefully kissed Livy's still-sleeping cheek and then stood over the bassinet where baby Nadia lay sleeping. He leaned down and took in the sweet smell of his newborn while reveling in the innocent sound of her breath as a slight newborn-smile could be seen in the faint light from the hallway. He gently brushed her cheek with a daddy's kiss and tiptoed quietly to Brock's bedside. As he knelt down to give his son a kiss on his forehead, he briefly stopped. Gazing at his beautiful boy, his heart was at once filled with pride and with dismay. Pride at what a blessing his son was to his life. Dismay at the lack of memories of such moments shared with his own father. But dismay quickly gave way to love and pride as Jake gently kissed his son goodbye and mouthed the words "I love you, son."

First class. He giggled at how far he had come. From a life of utter chaos, lower than low, to first class. As he marveled, he was even more grateful for the real riches he now experienced. The financial security of his job meant little to him in light of the richness of having a wife who loved him and fought for him and the children with which he'd been blessed. In spite of his struggles, life was good...and he was sitting in first class!

After hearing about first class from others in the office, he looked forward to the meal he would experience on the flight. Such was the simple pleasure of a man who secretly thought himself unworthy of such a lavish thing as a steak and baked potato served in midair at 550 miles per hour! Like a giddy little boy experiencing his first ice cream cone, Jake's mind and body were flooded with mood-changing endorphins even at the safety instructions given by the flight attendant! What a wonder this truly was in contrast to where he had come from! As the plane taxied down the runway and gently lifted into the crisp morning air, his mind was full of wonder and at peace. This would be a great day.

Even at the cruising altitude of 36,000 feet, Jake was mesmerized at the processes of the flight. While the plane was still climbing, the head flight attendant had come to him asking if he would prefer wine or champagne! As his wine was being poured, he was asked if he would prefer salmon or rib eye steak. Of course, he chose the dreamed-of rib eye! He anticipated the next question and blurted out, "Medium rare!" before the attendant even finished.

Laughing, she asked, "First time in first class?"

Jake replied, "Yes...and first time flying to be honest!"

Settling into his seat and sipping his red wine, Jake began to relax. He had never before imagined he could feel so good. So peaceful. So refreshed. So blessed. So lucky. Closing his eyes and thinking about Livy and Brock and little Nadia, he nodded off into oblivion as the aroma of salmon mingled with steak wafted throughout the cabin. After a few moments, he felt a slight touch on his shoulder. "Mr. Owens, lunch is served."

He was amazed at the lavish presentation now before him. A baked potato big enough for three, slathered with real, creamery butter steamed upward into his smeller. On one side of the massive china plate was a formidable serving of freshly steamed asparagus and a large fresh wheat roll. And there at center plate, just waiting for consumption, was that long-dreamed-of rib eye steak prepared just for him! And the pièce de résistance? A big piece of carrot cake. How could they have known it was his favorite?

Even amidst the faint roar of the jet engines, he could hear the sizzle of the steak and smell its wondrous aroma. Heaven! He must have died and gone to heaven. "How could life get any better?" he asked himself.

And then it happened.

Everything went silent.

Everyone went silent, numbed by the possibility.

There was no doubt. The engines no longer made a sound. And the sensation of forward motion was replaced with downward thrust as the plane's trajectory went from even to free-fall.

Jake's next thought? "What about my steak dinner!"

2

DENIAL

> Security is when everything is settled, when nothing can happen to you; security is the denial of life.
>
> GERMAINE GREER

"What about my steak dinner?"

Really?

It is said that the mind briefly goes numb when facing imminent death, and Jake's absolutely did. He didn't know it yet, but he was experiencing the first stage of grief. Everything around him told him he was about to die, but his mind argued that this was a normal occurrence. "The pilot will even the plane out in a second or two," he reasoned. His body told him one thing; his mind told him another. He had gone numb.

Jake was in denial.

Actually, he had been in denial many times in his short life. While he tried to reason a way out of the downward trajectory, he suddenly remembered something. He had felt this same feeling many times as a boy...as a teenager...as a young man in college. Before he knew it, he was no longer falling into thin air. He had fallen 25 years earlier when he was only five years old. And now he saw something that had haunted him for many years. Pushed back into the recesses of his psyche, like a festering wound that had never really healed anywhere but on the surface, he saw his little boy self in that old, musty basement again. The smell of wet, moldy soil filled his nostrils. He felt a sneeze coming on, but it gave way to the acute lack of color he recalled from the encounter. The gray. The black. The whiten of the white of the old man's eyes as his eyes adjusted to the dim light coming from the single window in the basement.

Old Man Winters, the weird next-door neighbor, had been around since Jake's earliest recollection. He was simply an odd codger, and Jake's mother had told him to "be careful around that old man." And he had been careful...at least as careful as a 5-year-old boy knows how to be. Mostly, Jake paid him no mind as he played in the backyard every day. Yes, he could tell when the old man was watching him, which was nearly every day, but that was the extent of it. He just watched while Jake played in the sandbox or tried to climb a little higher in the old mulberry tree that had grown into the chain link fence separating their two houses.

It all transpired innocently enough. While climbing the tree that day, he reached for that next branch—the one he had not been able to reach before. Just as his little hand made it to the branch, he lost his grip. He fell, knees absorbing the impact. Jake writhed in pain, clutching his now-bleeding kneecaps. Because he feared the wrath of his father, he tried not to cry too loudly.

By age five, he already understood that when his father was in a drunken stupor, like that day, the pain he felt in these bleeding wounds would pale in comparison to when his dad's belt buckle hit his naked behind. Even as he whimpered softly in the dirt, his fear overwhelmed him. Only recently, his dad had become so angry that he almost beat him half to death! His crime? Asking his mother for a cookie. She had said no, and Jake had cried. In response to Jake's tears, his dad grabbed his belt and ran madly at the boy, yelling, "You little bastard! Can you not see I am trying to sleep in here? This is my house and my food and I'm sick and tired of your pitiful little whine!" He grabbed his son by the hand, dislocating the boy's wrist while jerking him into the air, all while swinging wildly with the buckle end of his belt at his bare, bleeding legs. Jake was flung violently around the room as his father beat him, spit flying out of his profane mouth, his words as violent as the beating.

This would have gone on until his dad grew tired or passed out from his alcoholic rage had Jake's grandmother not stepped between them. Hearing the boy's anguished sobs from outside the house as she just happened to drop by to check on her grandson, Thelma Owens charged into the house to find her son beating her grandson mercilessly while her daughter-in-law lay in a stupor, having been slapped to the floor. Only when his dad's eyes locked with the eyes of his grandmother was the boy given a reprieve. "Owen Matthew Owens! Let him be! Let him be!" sobbed Thelma Owens to her son. As if awakened from a trance, Owen dropped the boy as quickly as he had jerked him from the floor. Jake could still see that look of shock on his dad's face as it melted into denial, gave way to eyes of shame, then just as quickly faded back into the look an addict gets when he's afraid. All he could say as he walked away was, "Keep the little bastard quiet. See what you caused, you little shit. Hell, no wonder I need a drink."

Jake saw all of this as the plane plummeted toward Earth, and he was reminded of the denial of that day just as he denied the happenings of this day.

That look—that fear of belittlement and beating—kept him quiet on the ground, knees bleeding, in such pain, that day. While trying to remain quiet, Jake didn't notice Old Man Winters. "You alright, boy?" he asked. Frozen in fear, Jake held his breath. As he tried to get up from the ground, the old man reached through the hole in the fence the tree had created through many years of growing through and stretching the chain link and said, "Let me see, son."

The old man gently lifted the boy's hands from his knees and took a handkerchief from the pocket in his overalls to wipe away the blood. As Jake's fear gave way to calm, his wounded heart began to flood with warmth he had rarely experienced in his short life. Someone touching him with nothing but care and concern.

Jake remembered how it felt to be valued by the old man. After a couple of minutes, the old man simply asked, "Would you like a cookie?" Nodding, Jake followed the old man into his house and down the rickety old staircase into that cold, dark, dank basement.

Funny, but falling from 36,000 feet did not cause him one iota of fear compared to what he felt that day in that basement. While he waited for the old man to come through with that promised cookie, Jake had figured out that if he wanted anything from life, it would cost him something. At least that's what he remembered feeling even if his beliefs were different now as an adult. Getting used to being berated and beaten into submission had caused him to not run when it happened.

The boy's eyes adjusted to the dim light and he noticed the whiteness of the old man's eyes reflecting from somewhere in the shadows. And his young eyes were drawn to something... down there. Why was the old man not wearing any clothes? Having seen his dad naked several times before had not prepared him for what the old man was asking him to do. Fearing being hurt, he simply did what was asked.

Falling fast, Jake recalled the smell. He remembered the need to throw up overwhelming him. He remembered not having a clue what was happening. He remembered the shame even though he did not know why he felt so ashamed. And he recalled the old man's words.

"This is our little secret...just between you and me,

boy...but if anyone finds out...well, I'm afraid something bad might happen to your mommy."

His mom. The one bright spot in his life. He could not let anything happen to her! So he kept the secret. Day after day. Week after week. Year after year. Trying to avoid the back yard, he was always somehow overpowered by the hidden things—or compelled in some way—by the old man for all those years right up until the day Old Man Winters died. It would take Jake many years of healing—or continued denial—before he dared share with anyone the horrors he had faced as a boy and as a young man.

While these images from the past swirled in his mind, Jake felt something near his face. And he could hear rushing air and plastic rubbing against plastic, all while feeling the sensation of falling. Or being pulled downward. Then his numbness gave way to sheer terror as he realized the oxygen mask had fallen from above his head.

Dangling there in front of his face, shaking along with the jet, were the emergency masks he had been warned about. He must have passed out because he never heard an announcement. And then it hit him: There had been no announcement. He had blacked out for a few seconds. And no one was saying a word. Not the pilot. Not the co-pilot. Not the flight attendant who had given the safety speech only minutes before. Not a single sound from a single passenger. Jake found this so odd. In his preparations for this very trip, he had allowed himself to imagine the fear and chaos that would ensue in just such a scenario!

But no one spoke, sighed, cried or even dared to breathe—or so it seemed. It was as if the entire group—from crew to passengers—had been reduced to mass shock in the moment of the downward motion of the plane. Eerily, all that could be heard was the constant rush of air as the plane and its contents continued to pick up speed and approach terminal velocity.

Could this really be happening? It didn't take long for denial to morph into feelings of utter isolation...like he was the only one experiencing what he was experiencing right now. He had known loneliness before. But not like this.

3

ALONE

> Loneliness expresses the pain of being alone and solitude expresses the glory of being alone.
>
> PAUL TILLICH

Trantex Airlines is known for its stellar safety record. That record seemed to be in jeopardy as Jake and 200 other passengers and crew of 6 aboard the Boeing 737 plunged to the ground. Jake had been so excited to take his seat—3B, in the aisle. Normally quite reserved and quiet, especially in new situations and environments, he'd been quite talkative to his seatmate.

Like a little boy playing with a new toy for the very first time, Jake had methodically gone over the buttons and fixtures of his seat. As was his custom when facing a new gadget, he had opened the manual. In this case, it was the in-flight magazine. He found the seat instructions near the back. He soon found the button on the armrest and pushed it, causing the compartment concealing the tray table to pop open, much to his delight!

Snickering, he hadn't noticed the tall, well-dressed man placing his briefcase and carry-on bag in the overhead compartment. He turned his attention to the small TV screen that had popped up from the other armrest and toggled to the screen that showed the map of the route the plane would take to Las Vegas. While his rapture continued, it was very apparent to the man as he stood there watching that Jake was new to flying.

"Having fun there?" asked the man.

Slightly embarrassed at his obvious oblivion to those around him, Jake jumped a bit, making the man laugh.

"It's my first time to fly...is it obvious?" asked Jake.

"Yes, but your joy is refreshing. And contagious."

Extending his right hand, the man said, "Hi, my name is Michael. Michael Manzon. And you are?"

Standing quickly, Jake promptly bumped his head on the overhead display panel. Cringing in pain and embarrassment, he nervously laughed and shook Michael's hand vigorously with his right hand while rubbing his bruised head with his left. Laughingly, Jake replied, "Awkward."

The two men struck up a conversation. Mostly small talk.

"What do you do?"

"I work for Nexus Texas. Design. And you?"

"I work for a world-wide organization called Monde Lumière. Benevolence. We raise money for fresh water wells in rural villages. We provide small business loans to developing economies. Mostly, my job is to get the word out about the mission."

Exchanging information, the two men settled in for the flight, Michael put on his noise-reducing headphones and nodded off. Jake continued his exploration of his surroundings. Such a pleasant and promising beginning to the trip. Such a good connection and possibility of an ongoing relationship.

Back to reality. Now both possibilities seemed incredibly short-lived. Jake glanced at Michael. To his amazement, he was still reclining, headphones on, eyes closed! Still unable to utter a word and not recognizing that he had not taken a breath for several seconds, Jake continued in and out of awareness. One moment he was falling with the rest of those on board. The next, he was somewhere else in time...at least in his mind. "I must be in shock, " he thought. "This must be some function of my body going in to self-preservation mode." Mostly, even though on a plane crowded with 200-plus people facing the exact same predicament, he felt alone.

How could one be so isolated yet surrounded by people? He had actually grown quite accustomed to it. In all those years of abuse at the hand of Old Man Winters, he had found it easier—and safer—to simply withdraw from life as much as possible. Even as a boy, his personality, extrovert, was tempered with the need to protect himself. Practically played out, rather than risk harming his mother, per the warning of Mr. Winters, he found it safest to keep to himself. While the other boys played and roughhoused around the neighborhood, Jake stayed in his room. On the days he dared to venture outside—usually days when the fear of his father's wrath overrode his fear of the other boys—the neighborhood boys would call to him to come and play. Due to his timidity, his reluctance to give himself fully to anything, they viewed him as...well...effeminate.

Even after the death of Winters, the die was cast, so to speak. Jake assumed this was just the way it was. That this was just the "way" he was. Loner. Safer alone. Maybe he really was not like the other boys. Maybe he really was different, as they said. The words of his dad were emblazoned on his heart: "Get out of the house, sissy boy! Go be a man like the other boys."

Rather than face the possible physical attacks and verbal bombardment—never mind the confusion of just exactly how one might be a boy and a man simultaneously—Jake found the treatment he faced in the outside world somehow more bearable than what he endured at home.

At first, he tried to do what his dad said. Venturing out, he was often teased. He did not even know what "fag" and "queer" even meant. But he knew, by the vitriol hurled his way along with these words, that it could not be good. When puberty hit, he got an inkling of what those terrible words meant and knew they did not truly apply to him. His first spontaneous erection at the sight of the hot girl in his sixth grade class had seen to that! Still, he found enduring the teasing mostly tolerable compared to his home life. And the fact that at least the other boys paid attention to him, that their teasing and treatment at least felt more like acknowledgment than anything he received from his dad, made him conclude that love was to be earned. Somehow.

And then there was school. To feel included in the brotherhood of boys, he had opted—actually forced by the school counselor out of necessity to maintain the proper amount of PE credits—to play basketball. It was somewhat less violent and less threatening than football, and he had grown to love it. Not because of camaraderie with the other boys but because it was something he could do by himself. Many times in his youth, Jake would sneak out of the house at night and make his way to the local park where, by the light of the lone streetlight next to the basketball court, he would shoot away the hours. Basket after lonely basket, between beatings, he played away while his dad lay in a drunken stupor at home. On more than one occasion, Jake had come home to face the wrath of his father who had discovered his absence when he yelled at Jake: "Bring me another damn beer, boy!"

His existence boiled down to knowing when to duck out of the way, honing his ability to hide in plain sight, and by coming to the conclusion—sadly—that to be beaten or teased or ridiculed or belittled was, at least, to be noticed. But that day in the locker room had shattered even that bleak reality.

After practice that day in sixth grade, the basketball team had all been told to "hit the showers," something Jake dreaded. Slow to develop, he had not yet grown hair "down there" like most of the other boys. Enduring the taunts, he had—at first—tried to hide his boy parts by cupping his hands over them in the shower. Of course, this only made the other boys that much more determined to point out his lack of development.

"Little boys shower over there!" shouted one of the seventh graders, pointing toward the shower on the far end of the wall, forcing Jake to walk the length of the shower room to the farthest of the six shower heads on either side of the room. While pointing to his own hairy balls, the older boy added, "Men shower here!"

Walking down the gauntlet of older boys was humiliating. Many were the days he had longed for his body to catch up to the other boys' bodies. As was his practice, Jake took his time in showering, making sure to be the last one left to avoid as much belittlement in the dressing area as possible.

Finally, the voices from the dressing room died down. Jake turned off the showerhead and waited, listening to make sure he was alone, and walked slowly and as silently as possible from the shower room to the dressing room. He opened his locker, where he'd left his towel and clothes, to discover—nothing! His clothes and towel were gone! And then he heard laughter.

"Did you lose something, sissy boy?" came the shout from outside the locker room.

"Give me my clothes, guys!" shouted Jake. "Please!"

"Whoa! Easy there, big fella!" came the reply. "Come and get 'em!"

Jake knew the boys would not bring him his clothes,

so he decided to simply wait them out. Surely the coach would come to check on the facilities and rescue him. Surely. After an hour, Jake horrifyingly concluded that help would not be coming. Sheepishly and slowly, he stuck his head out of the locker room door.

Gazing into the gymnasium, he could see his clothes in a pile beneath the basketball goal nearest the locker room. At least he would not have far to go. Seeing no one and hearing nothing, he burst from the locker room. The naked kid ran toward the pile of clothing. But just as he reached his clothing, the pile moved!

He had not noticed the fishing line wrapped around the bundle! Now an older boy pulled them farther out of his reach from the far end of the gym! He had not noticed, in his frantic running, the laughter coming from unseen voices! Now the entire seventh grade—boys and girls—jumped and ran from their hiding places around the gym! It was not until he saw the myriad flashes and glows from the smart phones filming his every naked move that true mortification and isolation took hold.

He curled up into the fetal position right there at center court. The ridicule and teasing had gone on for several minutes before a sixth-grade girl named Olivia heard the commotion from a nearby classroom where she had been working on an after-school project. When she saw what was happening, she ran to the pile of now-unattended clothes and rushed to Jake's exposed side. While she draped the boy's towel over him, she turned toward the mob and shouted, "How dare you! Stop it now!"

While she stood guard over Jake, the crowd continued to mock the boy. "Sissy boy needs a girl to come to his rescue! What a fag!" The crowd only dispersed when they heard that the custodian was about to come into the gym.

Jake didn't tell anyone in authority. He begged Olivia to keep the secret, telling her the less his dad knew, the better it would be for him.

Isolation. Loneliness. In that moment of lucid memory, Jake felt less alone riding to his death in a jet than he had felt that day in the gym. Turning his attention back to the falling, he saw that Michael was still sleeping. He asked himself, "Why is this taking so long?"

4

FREE FALL

> There are people who have too much space between their ears, and given the time, do nothing but free fall forever inside their head. It's a spooky thing to be left alone inside an angry inner-verse.
>
> JAMES ST. JAMES

How could Michael be sleeping when death was seconds away?! Oddly, this bothered Jake more than the reality of the moment! As he tried to get his voice to override the shock his body and mind were going through, Jake wondered if it would be better to awaken the man or to let him die not knowing it was coming! He laughed! But how could he be laughing when he would be dead in seconds?

He remembered the research he had done in the weeks prior to the flight. All his friends and business associates had found it incredible that Jake had never flown before. Why? It was simple: He'd never had a reason. He grew up near the place he went to college. He found work in the same city where he had gone to college. He had also never been able to afford it, finding driving much simpler. And then, of course, there was the fear factor!

The research. When Jake was told he was being chosen for the presentation in Vegas and that he would be flown there, he struggled about whether to tell his boss of the fear or simply bite the bullet. He had chosen to bite the bullet and to prepare himself for the flight. So he did research on flying—on air disasters and their frequency—to help alleviate his fears! And, at first, it did. The National Transportation Safety Board's statistics for 2008 showed only 20 accidents for U.S. air carriers operating scheduled service. This told Jake that, per million flying miles, there were, statistically speaking, zero accidents. And of those flying incidents that did occur, only five people were seriously injured during the studied period. And only one died! He reasoned that, since this was now 2018, airline safety standards had only gone up!

Compared to driving a car, traveling by air was statistically much safer. According to the National Highway Traffic Safety Administration, which compiles and researches accident statistics for the entire country, its 2008 Traffic Safety Facts Data boils down the millions of accidents and other statistics to 1.27 fatalities per 100 million vehicle miles traveled. Flying it would be!

Of course his research had not stopped with the basic statistics. Quite by accident, he had gone on to explore the possibility—just in case—of the survivability of an airplane crash.

And all that discovery now flooded his free-falling mind!

Now, numerous incidents of people surviving against all odds came coursing through his psyche! Like the story of the Serbian flight attendant, Vesna Vulovic. During a flight over Czechoslovakia, the DC-9 in which she served exploded in midair. Wedged between her seat, a catering trolley, the body of another flight attendant, and a ripped-away section of the aircraft, she and this section of fuselage had somehow managed to land on a snowy incline! Sliding down the incline for quite some distance before coming to a stop, she survived! Severely injured, but she lived!

And then there was Alan Magee. Alan had been blown out of his B-17 while on a bombing mission over France in 1943. Magee, from New Jersey, fell more than 20,000 feet to the ground! He crashed through the glass skylight of a train station and landed with a thud on the cold, stone floor. Nearby German soldiers, expecting to find a crumpled mass of flesh and bones, were astonished to find Magee had survived and summarily took him captive. It was reasoned that the glass had somehow slowed his descent enough to survive the sudden stop!

In his research, Jake found instances of people falling from great heights and living by falling into swampy soil, grassy fields, haystacks, and even trees! He also found that landing in water was equivalent to falling onto concrete. Just as concrete does not compress, neither does liquid! He began to run through the different scenarios he had found. Even though they had surely reached terminal velocity—somewhere around 120 miles per hour—due to air density and drag of the fuselage, the speed could possibly be reduced to a survivable rate.

He imagined ripping away his seatbelt and grabbing one of the blankets the flight attendant had allotted him during the pre-flight introductions and fashioning a makeshift parachute. Once the parachute was ready, he would open the cabin door just ahead and jump into the nothingness. He reasoned he stood a better chance of surviving in this manner than in riding out the ensuing crash of the plane he now found himself confined in!

Looking frantically around his seat for the blanket, his mind once again drifted to the still-sleeping Michael. How could he not wake up? He thought about the many conversations he had enjoyed with his well-intentioned friends concerning their own flying experiences.

Molly had warned him about obnoxious passengers. He could deal with anyone after all he had endured growing up in the madhouse he called home!

Matt had told him of the possibilities of hitting rough air—air pockets, he called them—and to remain seated with his seatbelt securely fashioned at all times unless he needed to go to the bathroom. Jake found this momentarily humorous, considering how perfectly Matt had quoted the flight attendant's safety instructions from his many years of flying experience.

Jim had regaled him with stories of his many skydiving experiences. Jake had chalked these up to mere half-truths designed to win a pissing contest with the other guys. But his other skydiving facts had a weirdly calming affect on Jake in the midst of this freefall. Jim had told him that, when skydiving, he spread his arms and legs to create drag and reduce his airspeed to around 120 miles per hour. If he tucked his arms and legs near to his body, he would drop like a rock nearing the 200 mile-per-hour range! Jake thought, "I won't tuck, that's for sure!"

His mind now reeled with the recalling of Jim's mini-seminar on air speed and terminal velocity. He had told him that the definition of terminal velocity was actually very simple: Terminal velocity is the constant speed that a free falling object eventually reaches when the resistance of the air through which the object is free-falling prevents it from further acceleration. In other words, when downward force equals upward resistance, acceleration stops. How this news might possibly help him now seemed oddly comforting in the weirdness of the moment. At least he knew what was happening!

He had begun falling in love with Olivia, his rescuer from the sixth-grade naked incident, the day it happened. While she comforted him as he lay in the fetal position, her angry glare at the offending students —and the news of the imminent appearance of the janitor—made them all scatter like the human roaches they were. While he struggled to put on his clothes, she discreetly turned her eyes and closed them while holding the towel between him and the main entrance to the gym. He loved her unwaveringly from afar from sixth grade on.

It would not be until they were seniors in high school that he dared to express any type of affection for her. But he had been in love—a love free fall, if you will—from that first day, hoping amidst despair that one day he could love her openly and freely as he dreamed might be possible. At least he had his dreams.

The recurring dreams he fell into every night of fitful sleep were of solace to his soul. For years, he assumed that the sheer frequency of the same dream, over and over, night after night, was confirmation of his impending insanity. No sooner would he fall into restless sleep than he was transported to a world unlike the one in which he actually lived. He supposed his dreams to be a direct reaction to and result of the books he read during the lonely hours in his room. He loved the tales of knights and dragons and kings and queens and bravery and loyalty. At least in his dream life, he felt stability. Even though captured by forces opposed to the king (who happened to be his father in those dreams) each and every night, his father—at least his dream-father—came to his rescue night after night.

Every morning was the same. Just as his dream came to a climax, he found himself about to be put to death by the evil lord of that particular dream. Without fail, each and every morning, he awoke feeling rescued. As if awakened on cue each morning at the moment of his rescue, the effect was one of hopefulness. He had sized this phenomenon up as sheer craziness. Yet one more thing he must conceal from others in order to maintain his safe distance.

Even as his mind drifted back to his current predicament, he thought of Livy and the kids. Of how wonderful life had been. His thought stuck there. How wonderful his life *had been.* Past tense. Thirty years? Thirty short years? Why? Why him? What would Livy do without him? How would his children grow up without his love? Would their lives be any better than the one he had lived in the house of his dysfunctional, emotionally distant dad? Would they remember him after a year? After five? After ten? Would Livy find another love? A better love?

The more he thought about these things, and Michael's oblivion to the danger, the angrier he became.

5

ANGER UNIVERSITY

> For every minute you remain angry, you give up sixty seconds of peace of mind.
>
> RALPH WALDO EMERSON

Man, was Jake angry! For a second, he let his mind run wild with it. He was angry with his mother. Why had she not done more to protect him from his dad's wrath and violence? Why had he even been born into such a lousy family? Why had life been so unfair to him? Why had he not been given a choice in the matter? In *any*thing? Of course, the anger at his dad was understandable, but Jake had allowed that anger to consume him. Even the thought of how angry he was at his father made him angry! And then there was the whole God thing. If God was really as big and good and loving and powerful as he had been told, why did He not do anything to change such a miserable life? And then there was Michael...

Since his meal had been served and the plane had begun its descent, Jake wasn't sure if time was advancing at Mach speed or passing painfully by in slow motion. In reality, all he had just relived in his mind had taken but a few seconds. Again he glanced over to see how Michael was responding to the situation. What he saw made him angry.

How could anyone sleep through such an ordeal? How could anyone be so passive in sheer terror? Surely Michael had simply had too much pre-flight wine, which made Jake want to let him sleep through it all. Better to die not knowing one is going to die than to watch it happen, he reasoned. Reason. There seemed to be no reason or rhyme to what was happening. This only added fuel to the flames of his angry heart, causing him to do as he used to: respond without rhyme or reason and lash out at whomever or whatever happened to be there. Even this realization—that he was simply responding the way his dad had always responded, that he was *just like his dad*—made him feel like he would finally explode!

How many times, especially when he was a boy, had Jake heard these words: "That's just the way you are, boy!" Growing up in an angry home had done its work on Jake, leading him to respond as he had been taught. In anger. There were even those rare moments of anger when he would lash out at his father, like the time he opened that birthday card from his grandmother and that brand new, crisp ten-dollar bill fell out! In his excitement, he made the mistake of showing his prize to his dad, who grabbed it and said, "I'll take that!"

"But dad, that's mine! Grandma gave it to *me*!" cried Jake.

"And who pays for this roof you live under? And who pays for all the meals you eat?" spewed his dad. Of course, everyone in the house knew Owen Owens could not hold a job for more than a few days and that Colette brought home the real bacon, which barely made ends meet. And any money she had not managed to hide from Owen was spent on booze. Just like when he took the birthday card, Owen Owens said it to his son on many occasions. "Son, you might as well get used to it. Anger is a part of life. Your old man, and my old man, and his old man...all angry. That's just who ya are. Deal with it."

Deal with it? How does one deal with something they believe to be part of who they are? Do they just go on barreling angrily through life roughshod over anyone unlucky enough to be in their way? What if a guy doesn't like who he is? What about change? Was it possible to be a man and not be angry? Jake had witnessed other dads from afar when he was growing up. What he had seen with his own eyes told him that maybe, just maybe, a man did not have to be angry. It's just that Jake had taken too many classes at Anger University and had learned well.

When puberty hit him with all its hair-producing, hormone-inducing force, he'd found himself at a crossroads in his own private world.

Just as his dad had not taught him the basic needs of manhood—like shaving—he had not taught him anything good about his sexuality. If it could be explained as such, one would have to conclude that Owen Owens had taught his son all the wrong ways to view his masculinity and real masculine sexuality.

Many were the nights Jake overheard his dad and mom having sex. From what he could gather, it was great for his dad and painful and unfulfilling for his mom. He could tell by his dad's grunts and groans that he was feeling something wonderful. But his mother's quiet sobs immediately afterward told him that she did not feel the same. Jake assumed this was "just the way it was," just as he assumed all the bad things about himself were "just the way it was."

Not long after his body began to develop, Jake started having urges. Urges to look at young ladies. Urges to look at any woman, for that matter. Urges he seemed to have no control over. Urges to touch himself. Urges so intense that the confusion he felt drove him to ask his dad—*his* dad, Owen Owens—to talk. One night when Colette was sent to the liquor store, Jake saw his chance. His reasoning? His dad always seemed to question his masculinity, so stepping out to ask his advice in that very area would be seen as "manly" to his dad. At least that was his hope.

"Dad," said Jake with a slight quiver in his now-changing voice.

"Humph?" grunted Owen.

"I need to ask you something?" said the boy.

"Ask me what?" replied Owen.

"About...you know...?" Jake answered, sheepishly.

"What the hell are you trying to say, boy? Just spit it out!" said his dad.

"I keep getting...you know...erections..." said Jake, almost under his breath.

"You keep getting what?" asked Owen, now sitting up from the recliner where he had been snoozing all afternoon.

"At night...when I'm asleep...and when I wake up...and when I see a pretty girl...I get... hard..." said Jake, now trembling.

His dad began to laugh uncontrollably, much to Jake's horror, but not to his surprise. "Don't play with it too much or you'll go blind!" Owen laughed. Jake wished he could crawl under the rug and disappear. He felt lower than low. He felt shame. He felt shamed. But his dad was not through. "If you want to be a man, you gotta do what ya gotta do, boy! Don't be such a fag. Just be a man. Grow a pair!"

Owen Owens had, once again, rather than helping out his son, confused him all the more. Since that day, knowing what he knew now, Jake understood that it probably would have been better for him had he never had that conversation with his dad. It had literally sent him over the edge.

As much to prove his masculinity as to mediate his own need for affection, Jake had begun a journey into promiscuity that eventually became a slow, downward spiral into near-insanity. All he heard from those around him was that he had no choice about how he felt. And feelings were everything.

From his very first awkward sexual encounter with that older girl in the darkness behind the bleachers that night during his seventh grade year, he would try to satisfy his very real need with very unreal encounters. More often than not, Jake would find himself saying all the right things—"I love you"—just to get what he wanted. No sooner had he completed his conquest than he felt that he had somehow used the girl. He felt shame. Shame in knowing he would not build any real relationship with her. Shame at being no better than his dad. Shame at how he then boasted about each conquest to the other boys in his small circle of friends. Shame at feeling he somehow had a right to hurt another person. Shame that what he was doing, no matter how much she seemed to enjoy it, was really hurtful in the long run.

With each encounter, Jake felt a bit more used up. With each moment of completion, he felt he had given away a part of himself he could never get back. The user eventually came to feel...used. He would try and convince himself that he deserved the sex. He would try to tell himself she had led him on. He would try to placate his conscience with the old excuse that everyone else is doing it. Shame began to accumulate to such a degree that, at times, the very thought of using another human being in the ways he had grown accustomed to actually rendered him unable to perform at all, which only sent him farther down the spiral of shame, which in turn only drove him to try all the more to conquer his masculinity by one more sexual conquest. And the anger he felt toward himself only made it worse, sending him deeper into that never-ending cycle of personal destruction. It seemed he had graduated from Anger U. right into the graduate work of self-loathing and unending shame.

Here he was, falling downward in a very literal death spiral, thinking about something he believed he had already dealt with. But he turned his thoughts to the moment Livy had come into his life. The anger, the shame, the self-loathing began to be replaced with soothing thoughts of healing, a lack of shame, a lack of guilt, a lack of turmoil, and a very real, life-giving relationship that began that first week of their senior year in high school.

Suddenly, Jake was startled right back to the sensation of helplessly falling. There was the steak, still sizzling on the plate. There was the baked potato, still steaming as the butter melted into its savory midst. And there was Michael, still sleeping away. Jake's mind, flying in so many different directions at once, seemed to be traveling faster than the falling plane. "How did I get here? Why is this happening? I am losing my freaking mind!"

His anger subsiding, Jake became a bit calmer and

began to conjure up ways to avoid the imminent crash. "Maybe we could glide to safety. If only I could remember what the glide ratio of a falling jet is...and could relay that information to the crew...to the pilot," he said to himself, as if they didn't already know!

Talk about losing his freaking mind.

6

THE PRAYER OF A DYING MAN

> We are dying from overthinking. We are slowly killing ourselves by thinking about everything. Think. Think. Think. You can never trust the human mind anyway. It's a death trap.
>
> ANTHONY HOPKINS

Since the dive began, a mere ten seconds had passed, but that made no difference to Jake. Simply acknowledging the free fall, coupled with the "owning" of his anger, caused Jake to spin headlong into a series of what ifs.

What if we can glide to a level position and skim across a body of water?

He had read somewhere in his pre-flight research that the glide ratio of a jet was something like 6:1, meaning that for every 1,000 feet of altitude it will glide another 6,000 feet. That was more than a mile! He recalled reading something about how each plane varied in its ability to glide when total engine failure had occurred. Something about angle of attack and airspeed and something else...like it made any difference to him now. What if, as he had read about a Canadian airliner many years before, the pilot could glide the falling plane to a nearby airfield, military or private or otherwise?

Like the ball in a pinball machine being flipped from point to point, his mind was constantly tilting from one thought to the next with such speed that, under normal circumstances, Jake would have been unable to discern one thought from the next. The human mind is capable of computer recall and velocity when necessary, or so Jake thought amidst the what ifs.

What if he could pull one of the life rafts from the overhead compartments he had heard about in the pre-flight safety presentation and then, somehow, use it just as Indiana Jones had done in *Indiana Jones and the Temple of Doom*? Should he inflate the raft before exiting the plane or should he wait and inflate it during the fall from the plane? Were they near enough to the Rocky Mountains so he could slide down the mountainside just as Indiana had done in his least favorite film of the Indiana Jones saga? Should he take back all the negative things he had said about the film through the years? What?

What if he could gather several blankets and somehow tie them together within the next few seconds and fashion a makeshift parachute? Would he help others do the same? What if the parachute only slowed him enough to preserve his life, yet not enough to prevent serious injury? Would the pain be worth the effort? What?

And why is everyone so quiet? Don't they know what's happening? Can't they see the oxygen masks flailing in their faces? Why do I feel so drowsy? Maybe I should put my mask on. Is it me or is it getting cold in here?

Of course, since Jake's perspective was based in terror, he had not realized that he, along with every other passenger and crewmember, was in shock. Adrenaline had kicked in and sent them directly into flight or fright mode. Since they were all hopelessly strapped inside of a giant rock with wings, flight had proverbially gone out the window and all that was left was pure fright.

What if this was all a silly dream, like those he had experienced as a boy? Surely he would wake up feeling rescued and have a good laugh! What a story he would have to tell. Would anyone believe the tale he had concocted was even possible? Would they reject it as implausible? Would he become a laughingstock? Why would anyone want to hear about a silly dream where everyone dies?

What if, in his last moments, he truly lost his mind? How would he even know since no one could read his mind? What if Livy and the kids were so devastated they could not go on without him? What if they weren't so devastated? What if Brock forgot about him? What if Livy found it easier to not tell newborn Nadia about her daddy out of concern for her developing a fear of flying? What if Livy remarried? What if all he had experienced in life had not been worth it? Had his life been worth it?

So clouded with questions, he felt like he was being charged with a thousand lightning bolts all at once. Would his mind be able to withstand the constant cacophony of questions before it short-circuited? How could he keep from losing it completely? And then, not knowing what else to do, he began to pray...out loud.

"Lord, are you there? Maybe a better question is 'Are you here?'"

In that moment, all he could hear was the whistle of a jet plummeting to Earth.

"If you're here, can you help me?"

Silence.

"Would you get the plane's engines started again?"

Nothing.

"Can you at least give the pilot the wisdom he needs to fix whatever's going on here?"

The sound of wind against wings.

"If you help us, I will never cuss again." Still nothing but at least Jake felt a bit better about himself, imagining God might be swayed by his stellar performance or at least his desire to be better. To do better.

"If you get me out of this mess, I will never lash out in anger again."

The more he bargained with God, the better Jake felt, as delusional a way of thinking as it was. Bargaining with God had never worked before. Why did he think it might work now? Desperate people tend to do—and think—desperate things regardless of how futile they are.

Jake continued to lay out his pleas before the silent God. On and on went the whistling wind. The more he bargained, the more his memory took him back to all the other times he had bargained with God. His family had never been much for church, save for the public appearances his dad forced them to make every Easter and Christmas. Jake's perception of God was as skewed as his dad's had been. If God was real, He did not seem to care for him. If God was real, He didn't do anything about Jake's family situation.

Jake had cried himself to sleep as a boy after one particular Christmas Eve service the family had attended. He recalled the wonder he felt as he watched the children portray shepherds watching their flocks. He remembered how a group of angels announced the birth of someone they called baby Jesus to those same shepherds and how three of the wisest men of those ancient times had sought to bring extravagant gifts to the newborn baby. He had been mesmerized by the message the narrator kept conveying—that God so loved the world he had sent his very own son to save it from something called sin.

The more the story unfolded that night and the more he thought about the images he had seen, the more he wondered what it could mean to his messed up life. If this God they spoke of was real and as powerful as they said, if he was anywhere nearly as loving as they portrayed him to be, why was he not powerful enough to intervene in his life? And then there was that Easter when the church they visited performed a play in which baby Jesus was all grown up. He was whipped and killed on a cross but supposedly rose again. And, just as at Christmas, Jake wondered why a God that could raise His dead son from a grave was not powerful enough to do something about his predicament.

In a sense, all Jake had known of God and the teachings of the Bible—the weird, old book everyone at the church talked about and carried with them—made about as much sense as the superhero comics he used to read under the covers by flashlight in bed. Superman and Batman and all the others made him feel that maybe, somewhere, somehow, someday someone would come along and rescue him like those that always seemed to be rescued in his beloved comics. In Jake's young mind, God was merely another superhero. He hoped he was real, but his very real existence communicated quite the opposite. Still, he found himself crying to sleep after that Christmas Eve service. Now, as he and the other passengers hurtled through the air, he remembered the first prayer he ever prayed.

"God...if you are real...I really need you to help me...to help my dad to stop hurting me and my mom...to help my mom to not have to work so hard...to help my dad stop drinking...to help me not get teased so much."

He had waited a few minutes to see if anything happened. And nothing happened. He reasoned, having learned to do this with his dad, that if he promised to do something better or have a better attitude or to do something that his dad would really be pleased with, then God would come through with whatever it was he was asking for. Even though his dad never ever came through on anything he promised. Still, superhero God might be different.

"Maybe I asked for too much, God. Just help my dad get better...if you'll do that, I won't ever lie to my dad again...and I'll obey my mom better...I promise." Again he waited. And again, nothing happened. From that night on, he still looked forward to those Christmas and Easter church shows, putting as much faith in the God they sang and spoke about as he put in those comic book characters. At least hope in a cartoon—or a distant all-powerful being—was something to dream about. And even those simple dreams from that Christmas Eve stayed with him through the years. Jake's perceptions of God were a direct result of how he perceived his father's interaction with him just as his dad's only interaction was when he needed Jake to do something for him or when he was disciplining him for yet another mistake. In his mind, God was about as dependable as Owen Owens.

Just as Jake had played the what ifs—a sort of bargaining with his own mind—he had bargained with God all those years, never seeing one iota of evidence of God's existence in his life. As the plane hit a gust of wind from the jet stream they were now passing through, he was startled back to the present. In sheer frustration, he shouted, "Help me, God! If you help me, I will do whatever you ask!"

Rushing wind was all Jake heard in reply and his heart sank. "Please, God. If you're there, can you please do *something?*"

At that very moment, Michael woke up and looked Jake square in the eye. With a grin from ear to ear—the weirdest grin Jake had ever seen—he said, "Pray like that all you want, Jake. It's nothing but a practice in futility. You might as well give it up. Deal with it."

While Michael reclined his seat, Jake was at once appalled at and bewildered by the words of his seatmate. Amidst the roar of the wind outside the airliner, as the aroma of freshly served steak and baked potato wafted through the cabin, Jake began to weep. Overcome with despair, all he could think about was everything he was about to lose: his wife, his babies, everything. Not to mention the tears he wept over his impending death.

7

LIVY

You can't blame gravity for falling in love.

ALBERT EINSTEIN

"Deal with it?" Had Jake heard him correctly? "Deal with it?"

Anger overtook him along with the pangs of both incredible self-pity and debilitating fear. Crying tears of depression-fueled rage, he violently shook Michael by the shoulders.

"What do you mean 'deal with it'?" asked Jake. "I seem to be the only one on the whole damn plane actually dealing with it!"

"How is this any different than any other moment of your life?" asked the eerily calm Michael.

"Are you crazy, man? Have you lost your freaking mind? We are all dying here!" shouted Jake.

"Again, how is this moment any different than any other time in any of our lives?" asked Michael.

Tears streaming, incredulity burning from his eyes toward Michael, Jake could now hear the faint whimpers of other passengers. "Finally," he thought. "Everyone is coming to their senses." The whimpers grew louder. Some turned into screams. And those screams melted into wails of sheer horrifying terror as all on board realized that they were about to die.

While mothers fumbled to place oxygen masks on terrified toddlers and newlyweds clung together in their last embrace; while the Catholics crossed themselves and Hail Marys were hurled into the air; while screams of "Allahu Akbar" flew about intermittently between the pathetic cries of grown men screaming like little girls; while many still sat motionless, frozen in fear; while an old lady sang a faint quivering version of Amazing Grace, Jake just stared at Michael.

"You're nuts, man! I don't know about you, but I'm not gonna give up that easily!"

Jake fumbled for his seatbelt buckle, and Michael looked at him again. This time, as if piercing a place in his soul Jake had never let anyone see before, Michael asked, "What would Livy say? What would she do if she were here right now? Listen, Jake. What would she say?"

Why would he dare bring Livy into this? How did he know his wife's name? For the life of him, he could not recall mentioning her name in their earlier conversations. Before Jake could respond, his memories once again sent him into a time-stand-still trance as he saw himself back in high school. Having gained quite the reputation as a player among the females at school, Jake had hit a dry spell relationally, not that anything close to real honest relationship had ever been a reality for him. Relationship, to Jake, had been getting what you can and moving on...just as he had learned at home. It was as if the word had gotten out that he was nothing more than a user. He knew this to be true as he had inadvertently overheard some of the girls talking behind the bleachers in the gym as he lay above them ditching yet another class. It was the giggles that first caught his attention. Quietly turning his ear toward the opening beneath the seat he was laying down in, he heard the entire conversation.

"I heard you went out with Jake Owens," said the first girl.

"Are you kidding me?" the second girl replied. "You'll never find me giving him as much as the time of day."

"But I thought you liked him?" asked first girl.

"He only wants one thing...and he only wants it one time. I'm not gonna be the next notch on his pathetic belt."

That was enough. Jake swore off dating that day. At least he tried. Temptation always seemed to get the best of him. The more he indulged in his sexual passions, the more his reputation as a user grew. Soon, most of the ladies avoided him. Not merely avoided him, but actually shunned him. He had hurt quite a few girls. Broken more than his fair share of hearts. Wounded those he thought he was loving. Damaged the ones he sought out to help bandage the wounds in his own heart. Jake was messed up. Damaged goods. He felt more worthless than ever. He no longer needed his dad's emotional abuse to tell him so. He knew he was a loser. His very existence told him that.

And then came Livy.

It happened not long after the overheard conversation in the gym. Walking down the hallway between classes, Jake was used to almost every girl turning her back to him. But she didn't. In fact, she smiled at him. He had seen her before. That day he was left naked in the gym and she had come to his rescue. That day he had fallen in love with her but had stuffed the possibility of ever being with her in a distant place in his heart. But since then, he had avoided her like the plague in order to evade the teasing of the other boys. He had few male friends—and even fewer female friends. He had gladly lost touch with Olivia Jones since that dreadful and had heard rumors of the beautiful but weird virgin girl they called Livy but had never put two and two together. Livy was Olivia. She was one of "those girls." A virgin. He had heard other boys recounting their many failed attempts at dating—hooking up with—her. That she would even smile at him caused a longing to stir in his heart. He wanted her. His body needed her.

"Hi, Jake," was all she said...and she had him by the heart!

That someone like her would take the time to even acknowledge someone like him made him feel something he hadn't felt much in his life. Worth. Of course, he had briefly felt similar feelings whenever his grandmother had hugged him. His grandmother Owens always made him feel special. When he was with her, he felt he could conquer the world. When he was with her, he somehow believed her when she told him, “There is no one more precious on this earth.” Even the grandmotherly pride she exuded when he was younger often carried him through hard times as a teenager. “Don’t let anyone tell you you can’t do something, Jake. You can do and be anything you want to be. Just believe.” It had been quite some time since he had felt anything resembling worth to another human being. After all, his grandma Owens died when he was thirteen. Once again, abandoned. At least his grandmother had an excuse. Death was the ultimate separation but easier to swallow than living in a house where actual human beings lived together yet acted as if the others didn’t even exist...except when they needed something from you!

“Hi, Jake! Is anyone in there?” Livy giggled.

“Oh...uh...hi,” was all he could get out.

“I’m Olivia—Livy. Livy Jones,” she went on.

“I know who you are, but how do you know me?” he asked, pretending he did not recognize her.

“I’m one of those people that enjoys getting to know new people. And you’re ‘new’ to me,” she said with a confidence Jake thought could be either arrogance or sincerity. As she went on, he felt embarrassed to have judged her as anything but sincere. What he had not seen that day was that she respected him enough to not bring up the naked incident.

"Me and a group of my friends are getting together at Early Rush—the coffee shop down on Main."

"Oh, yeah," he replied. "I know where that is, but I'm not much of a coffee drinker."

"That's okay. I'm not either. I just enjoy being with my friends, and I'm always looking for new friends! Seven o'clock tonight?" she asked.

"Uh...sure...I'll see if I can be there. I'll need to check in with my folks," he lied.

Jake knew his dad would never miss him and that his mom would be glad for her son to be anywhere but in the danger zone called home.

And little did Jake know, but Livy—and seemingly everyone else—knew of his rough home life. He would be grateful for the time away from home and looked forward to getting to know Livy, who was no longer that gangly, skinny rescuer from seventh grade. As much as his relational experience to that point in his life would allow, he really did want to know her in a deeper way than just sex.

He arrived at the coffee shop a bit early and slinked into a corner. His goal? To check out Livy's friends before he ventured into whatever weird conflagration of people he might encounter. There was Livy, seated on a couch in the far corner with her back to the front entrance. Two girls were first to make their way to Livy. He had seen them at school but could not remember their names. Next came Bradley Palmer, a guy from his math class. One of those who always raised his hand with the right answer. You know, the ones no one else can stand, the one who has been on the receiving end of many a wedgie! And then he rolled his eyes when Sara McIntosh came through the door and made her way to Livy's couch. The word around school was that she and her friends were "holy rollers"—weird religious freaks, to be avoided. And Livy was one of them? Jake got up and skulked stealthily toward the front entrance just in time to hear Livy say, "Jake! Jake! We're all back here!"

Red-faced and fearful at being seen with one of these freaks, Jake simply waved and left. But before he even made it to the end of the block, he heard his name again. "Jake! Hey, Jake! Wait up!" He turned to see Livy trotting his way. "Where you going?" she asked.

"I...er...uh...I forgot. My dad needs me to mow the lawn," was the best lie he could think of in the moment.

"This late? It'll be dark soon," she reasoned.

Knowing a bit about Jake's situation at home and not wanting to embarrass him, she wisely but firmly said, "Jake, it'll be okay. My friends won't bite."

"Let's be honest, Olivia...Livy...it's kinda obvious I'm nothing like your friends. Let me save us all a ton of time and trouble. I'll just go home. I'm just not into the religious God thing."

Not easily deterred, Livy gently touched his shoulder, looked him in the eye and said, "Just come back in and meet them...and if, after a couple of minutes, you don't feel comfortable, I'll help you make your escape.

And just so you know...this is not some religious God thing. It's just coffee." Winking her eye in that "How can I say no to that?' way he would come to know and cherish in later years, he caved.

"Okay. A couple of minutes," he said.

Little did he know that his life would be forever changed by the series of events set in motion in that coffee shop with a bunch of weirdos!

8

CHANGE

> If you change the way you look at things, the things you look at change.
>
> WAYNE DYER

After that night at the coffee shop, Jake spent more and more time with Livy and her friends. Even though he always felt self-conscious—inwardly he felt like such a fake—he felt something he had only dreamed of feeling since he was a boy: Simply knowing and being known. Sure, it was only as deep as his first layer of thick skin. He didn't even know what to call this feeling until later...the feeling of belonging, coupled with the feeling of being needed.

As the plane fell from the sky, Jake went deeper and deeper into the recesses of his memory to the time his dad had finally caved on something 6-year-old Jake had asked and asked for. His dad had done it out of shame over the latest beating he had given to his wife and son. Jake didn't care. There it was! A little, fluffy, mass of black and white and brown fur! A puppy! His dad bought him a puppy! Owen probably found the little thing at the local Walmart where people often parked their trucks on Saturdays, tailgates down, pickup beds full of puppies and kittens of all shapes and breeds and sizes, each truck adorned with a sign saying, "Free Puppies." Again, Jake didn't care. He had a puppy!

That very first night had set the tone for the few short weeks of that puppy's life. Jake cradled the little furry ball of life in his arms as he ran into his room. Finding a towel from the pile of dirty clothes in the corner, he fashioned the "she-pup," as his dad had called her, a makeshift bed right next to his. For the next hour, Jake played and cuddled and wrestled and laughed out of sheer joy. He felt a connection to another living thing that required nothing of him but love and attention. The more he loved on that little pup, the more she licked and yelped in glee, nipping playfully at his fingers and licking the boy all over his frozen-in-a-smile face!

"What should I call you? I know. I'll call you 'Happy' 'cause you're so happy!" Content as he had ever felt, Jake put Happy to bed in the towel and crawled into his own. As puppies newly weaned from their mothers usually do, Happy began to whine...and whine...and whine...until the door to Jake's bedroom flew open and Jake's dad rushed in with a rolled up newspaper and began to beat the little puppy. The terrified little fur ball began to yelp and run around the room, unable to get out of the reach of the giant assailing her. Finally, Happy ran under Jake's bed, hiding as far away from the pain as she could.

"Boy, keep yer damn dog quiet or I'll do it for you! If I hear her again, she's gone, I can promise you that!" yelled Owen Owens. "Get under there and get her out!"

Jake scrambled beneath his bed and scooted his way to the farthest corner where he could just make out Happy's shining eyes. She whimpered in fear. As the boy reached out his hand to comfort her, she withdrew as far as she could from him. The same little puppy that had just minutes before been frolicking around the room in pure joy was now reduced to paralyzing fear. It had taken Jake longer to get the puppy than his dad's patience thought necessary, so he reached beneath the bed and grabbed his son by the ankle and said, "Grab her, damn it!"

Afraid that he might receive the same lashing his puppy had just received, Jake grabbed Happy. Out of self-preservation, the little puppy bit into the boy's hand, causing Jake to cry out, "Ouch!"

He responded in kind, slapping the dog across her little face. This only caused her to yelp again and jerk around in Jake's arms. While Owen dragged the boy from beneath the bed, the puppy continued to struggle against Jake. "Listen, boy! Either you keep her quiet or she goes in the shed!"

For the next two weeks, this was a nightly routine. After that second week, though, Happy was not happy anymore. In fact, not only did she cower in fear whenever Owen was near, but she also began to cower whenever Jake was near. Owen threw Happy into the shed at the end of the second week. Jake followed his dad into the night, clad only in his underwear, begging, "Daddy, no! Daddy, please! You're hurting her!"

Owen threw the puppy through the door while applying a firm backhand to his crying son's face. While Jake lay on the ground, he watched his dad latch the shed door. "Leave her there, boy. In fact, don't let her out until she's learned her place," Owen said.

For the next two weeks, the little boy went to feed and play with his puppy every day, only to find her hiding in the corner farthest from the door. She no longer came to the food dish when Jake fed her. She no longer responded with anything even approaching happiness. Day after day, she loved less and less until the day he went to the shed and found Happy lying still in the darkness.

While his dad begrudgingly dug a hole in the yard, away from the house, he berated his son. "This is what I get for trying to make you happy. You can't even take care of a stupid puppy! Why did I ever think you could? Damn, boy!" While he walked away, Owen ordered his son to "Put her in there and cover her up...then get yer sorry ass back in the house and get cleaned up for dinner."

Jake placed the dirt over his dead puppy and quietly made his way into the house and, like Happy, skulked as quietly as he could out of fear of awakening the beast he called dad. He washed his hands and came obediently to the dinner table, but he didn't eat. Even after the gentle and panicked urging of his mom, Jake would not...could not...eat. In fact, he could not even bring himself to look at his dad or his mom. His dad's response? "This ends tonight, you little peckerwood!"

Owen jerked his son up from the table, walked him to the hallway closet and threw him in. "Stay there until you're ready to act like a human being!"

Jake sat there in shock for the next few minutes until his dad returned with his untouched plate of food and slopped it down on the closet floor. He then slammed a cup of water next to the plate, sloshing most of it onto the floor, and closed the door. He numbly listened to his father's footsteps fade away and heard him yell, "Woman! You leave him be until he learns his place around here."

"But Owen, he's just a boy!"

Jake heard his mother's body slam against the wall in the hallway as his dad's backhand met her face. "If he ever wants to be a man, he's gotta learn now! This is a man's world, not a wuss's world! If he's not gonna talk to us, we ain't gonna talk to him!"

For the next week, Jake's only contact with his parents was when they opened the door to feed him or give him water. Or when Jake's dad threw in the mop bucket along with a half-gone roll of toilet paper, saying, "Piss in that! And wipe yer ass when you're done, boy." After three days, Jake's shock wore off and he began to cry. "Momma! Let me out...Please!"

Nothing.

Jake would not find out until years later that his dad had threatened his mother's life if she so much as spoke to him. This silent treatment had gone on for seven days and was broken only by Owen's selfish demands. Having ordered his wife to the store for a bottle of whiskey meant Owen had no one to serve him.

"Where is my food, woman?"

The drunk opened the closet door. He grabbed his startled boy by the arm and jerked him to his feet. Jake squinted at the sudden burst of light. "Get out here and get me some food, boy!"

As Jake stumbled toward the kitchen, his dad's right foot land squarely on his bottom, sending him crashing to the floor in tears. "And stop yer cryin', you little faggot! Fix me a sandwich!"

Trying to squelch his tears, Jake got up to find his dad's fist cocked and ready to strike him. He instinctively threw his arms up to protect himself, and his dad laughed. "Say something, boy."

"Thank you," was all Jake could say as he scurried to the kitchen.

Thank you? As Jake looked back on that episode, he recalled being thankful that at least his dad had spoken to him. At least his dad had touched him, even if it was a sudden, violent jerk and a swift kick to the rear. At least...

His mind swirled with the horrible memory, and then Jake suddenly found himself remembering another moment, at the front door of the Jones residence. Even before his nervous, shaking finger could push the button to ring the doorbell, Livy opened the door. "Jake! Come in!"

Jake was struck at the home's simplicity. Expecting a lavish interior, he had assumed that people who lived on that side of town would be a lot more extravagant. Livy closed the door behind him and extended her hand for Jake to follow her, saying, "Come with me, Jake. I want you to meet my family."

They came to the kitchen where several people were gathered around the center island, talking and laughing. Suddenly, the group grew quiet. After a moment of awkward silence (awkward to Jake, but to no one else), Livy said, "Hey, everyone. This is my friend, Jake!"

Before Jake could even get out a nervous "hello," Livy's mom rushed to embrace him! While she squeezed the lanky teenager, he just stood there frozen, not knowing how to respond. "Welcome, Jake! We've heard so much about you! I'm mom...but you can call me Linda!"

Still reeling from the unexpected affection, Jake had been blindsided by Livy's dad. Being accustomed to bear-hugging his children—sons and daughters alike—Max Jones reached for Jake. Before he could catch himself, Jake found himself recoiling from the big, burly man...in fear!

Although he was indeed big and burly, Max Jones had lived a hard life and understood the boy's reaction. Sensitive to not cause any further humiliation, he simply extended his hand. Once Jake understood what was happening, he returned the older man's gesture and shook his hand vigorously. Before Jake knew what hit him, Max took him by the right hand and pulled him into his shoulder, giving the boy a gentle man-hug. Jake's mind was at war with itself in that moment. In a split second he was abhorred by and consumed with fear, recalling all the times he had been touched by his dad in anger, while also feeling so overwhelmed by something he had only imagined possible.

As Jake's fear gave way to the embrace of Max Jones, he felt protected, not alone. Wanted.

Before he knew what was happening, Jake began to cry. Uncontrollably. There in the Jones family kitchen, he fell apart and felt safe to do so.

9

FALLING APART

> The rate at which a person can mature is directly proportional to the embarrassment he can tolerate.
>
> DOUGLAS ENGELBART

> Honesty is grounded in humility and indeed in humiliation, and in admitting exactly where we are powerless.
>
> DAVID WHYTE

Jake was in an emotional free-fall...aside from the fact that his plane was plummeting to Earth. Like dust in a tornado, his thoughts were swept up and back to that very moment in the Jones' kitchen. How was it even possible to be completely embarrassed—humiliated—because he was falling completely to pieces in front of complete strangers? In front of Livy—the one person he quasi-trusted? How could he feel both humiliation and safety at the same time?

The human mind in moments of stress can seem profoundly incapable of coherent function while simultaneously performing the function of thought at seeming light speed. Feeling profound fear yet laughing at the absurdity of his situation while reliving a past event caused him to both cry and chuckle. Random thoughts like "Why me?" juxtaposed with "I am no different than anyone else on this flight. We are all dying." His mind ping-ponged like lightning between present and past...and past was somehow winning the moment.

Max Jones held the boy for the next 20 minutes, so intense was the release of the many years of pain. Jake felt then like he was losing his mind but later remembered feeling nothing but freedom. Tears fell like a deluge of rain and brought with them cleansing and a weird kind of hopefulness only a man who realizes he's at the bottom with no place left to go but up feels. Somehow Jake felt all those things at the same time.

Owen Owens despised tears. "Real men don't cry" had been his oft-spoken and well-understood motto. Of the many instances in his childhood when that motto had been played out, the one that came to mind in that kitchen that fateful day blared like a heavy metal song in his psyche.

He vividly remembered the day his grandma Owens surprised him at age 7 or 8 with a secondhand bicycle she found at a local garage sale. Jake didn't even know what secondhand meant. All he saw was a dream come true! He had learned better than to ask his dad for anything after the puppy incident or at least to be very careful of the timing and attitude he portrayed when asking. So he had planned on waiting until Christmas to ask his dad for a bike. But that year, Christmas came early!

While his grandmother and mom, Colette, watched from the front porch, Owen, obviously hung over from the previous night's binge, arrogantly said, "I'll teach the boy to ride. Come here." His mind full of wondrous thoughts, Jake shyly edged toward the bike with great reverence. Excited to have received such a gift, Jake thought he would be happy just to step back and look at the bike for an hour or two. He had already decided where he would store it in the garage, how he would care for it, what he would say to anyone who asked if he had a bike. "I have a Schwinn!" he would say. He had not even gotten to so much as touch the bike and now his dad was telling him to get on.

Jake remembered the look in his dad's eyes that day. A look he had not seen much—if ever—before. He saw something akin to what Jake felt. Joy! Jake could only imagine his dad must have dreamed of the day he could teach his son how to ride a bike. After all, Jake had felt the same way about Brock. And Jake recalled seeing something else that day: A glimpse of pride gleaming in his dad's eyes. Good pride. The pride that says, "This is my son! He's gonna ride a bike and I'm gonna teach him!" Jake's fear of failing gave way to one of those rare moments—if not the only one—of feeling his dad's pride and belief in him. It made him feel like he could fly! Or at least ride a bike!

While Owen steadied the bike for his son, Jake straddled the seat. The seat that was a bit too high for his legs. He put his hands on the handlebars and exhilaration flooded his entire body! "Now, put your feet on the pedals, son." He could hardly believe his life in that moment. He had dreamed of having a bike! He had dreamed of riding like the wind through the neighborhood! And now he was about to realize his dreams! While his dad pushed him forward, Jake felt the adrenaline coursing through his veins. Confidently gripping the handlebars, he obeyed his dad's command. "Pedal, son!"

Like the sensation of flying you get when the plane lifts off the ground is how Jake felt when his dad let go! How glorious he felt! How invincible he felt! How proud he felt!

Then the unthinkable happened. Jake's confidence began to wobble in time with the wobble of the handlebars. His joy was replaced with sudden, paralyzing fear as the mailbox loomed near. His pride was dashed to shreds as he crashed into the mailbox. Just as the left pedal made contact with the post, the sudden stop and awkward angle slung Jake's head directly into the mailbox, sending the boy flying from the seat and onto the sidewalk. He landed on both knees and crumpled to the ground in tears. While his son lay humiliated and bleeding from the palms of both hands and the caps of both knees, Owen Owens lit into him.

"Stop your crying, boy! Get up and get back on!"

Fearing his dad's wrath more than the pain he now felt, Jake tried to get back up but winced in pain.

"Dad, I can't!"

"You're gonna get back on this bike right now or I'm gonna give you something to cry about! Don't embarrass me! Look, boy! The whole neighborhood is watching."

And it was true. Several of the neighbors had come to see what was going on. He had wished that just this once his dad had helped him. Tended his wounds. Asked if he was alright. Simply held him.

And all those memories burst through the dam of his heart and spewed out on the shoulders of Max Jones that day. Like a volcano that had built up so much pressure that the lava of hurt had finally reached the surface, Jake wept. It was as if he had finally had a wound surgically cleaned—a wound that had required surgery long ago but had only been covered with a Band-Aid. Jake's heart had been effectively lanced and the hurt and agony and sorrow and suffering he had endured poured out.

Covered in Jake's tears and snot, Max didn't recoil. Jake's uncontrollable wails of release piercing his ear was of no consequence to Max Jones. While Jake fell apart, Max held him together. And the more Jake cried, the tighter Max's grip became. This "love-grip," as Jake would later call it, only induced a greater release in Jake and the tears became intertwined with wailings as the boy began to vomit out memory after memory, wound after wound.

"My dad's a drunk...and he beats my mom...he beats me!" sobbed Jake.

"I know, son. I know," said Max gently.

"All I've ever heard is how much of a loser I am! How much of a faggot I am! How much a disappointment I am! How 'nothing' I am..." His voice trailed off in unintelligible sobs.

"I know, son. I know."

"What is so wrong with me? Why am I such an idiot? Why did he have to be my dad? Why does my mom never stand up to him? Why am I so worthless? Why can't someone just love me for me...for who I am?" wailed the boy.

"You are not an idiot," Max calmly began. "You are not worthless...and you are loved."

At that one statement—you are loved—Jake grew suddenly quiet. Stunned that it could remotely be true. He waited...but not for long.

Max broke the silence. "I love you, son."

Jake buried his head even deeper into Max's shoulder—if that was even possible—and sobbed again. "Why has my dad never told me he loves me? Why could he not say just one good thing about me? What is so damn hard about that?!"

Max waited patiently for the boy to get it all out of his system. When the tears finally subsided, he gently took Jake by the shoulders and turned him so the boy could see directly into his eyes and said, "Jake, hurt people hurt people."

"What does that even mean, Mr. Jones?" asked Jake.

"I know this will sound crazy to you... but...have you ever wondered why your dad lashes out at you beyond it being your fault?" asked Max.

"What do you mean?"

"Jake, I'm not excusing the behavior of your dad toward you, but something I've come to know is this. When a man is wounded—deeply wounded—and gets no healing for that wound, all he knows is how to wound. I would bet your dad was wounded by his dad and never got his wounds dealt with. He's just done to you what was done to him. Reality is simple, Jake. Your dad is tangled up in a big mess of stinkin' thinkin' about himself. You can end the mess as far as your life is concerned right now. If you'll let me—let us—we will help you learn to untangle your own mess. Jake, have you ever heard the story of Wrong Way Corrigan?"

"Wrong Way Corrigan?" Jake repeated.

"In 1938, a pilot named Douglas Corrigan set off to fly from Brooklyn, New York, to Long Beach, California and wound up in Ireland."

"You're kidding!" said Jake.

"Not kidding!" laughed Max.

"Some say it was all part of a navigational error while others thought it was an intentional "mistake" since his requests for authorization to make the transatlantic flight had all been denied. For the sake of my analogy, let's assume it was a navigational error. You, son, have made some navigational errors...some wrong choices in life. Jake, your reality can be changed by the choices you make."

"But I had no choice in who my dad would be!" Jake replied.

"That is true, but you always have a choice as to how you will respond to your dad and even how you will respond to crappy circumstances. Just as with Wrong Way Corrigan, who turned a very dangerous navigational error into a positive, I can help you...if you'll let me...turn your navigational errors into positives."

Jake remembered feeling that what Max was saying was too good to be true, but at the same wondering what he had to lose. Funny, but the feeling that overrode all others that day was ironic, to say the least. Jake felt like a man who had just jumped out of a perfectly good airplane...without a parachute!

10

WRONG WAY, RIGHT WAY

I have woven a parachute out of everything broken.

WILLIAM STAFFORD

When Max Jones offered to help him untangle the mess of his life, Jake felt hope. Yet he knew he was about to enter uncharted territory—like falling from 10,000 feet without a parachute! He played back the wonderful memories of that day in the kitchen of Max Jones: his head buried in the man's shoulder, Wrong Way Corrigan ... then the theme song to Gilligan's Island began to play in his mind.

Owen, in moments of lucidity, used to watch reruns of the old TV show, often allowing Jake to watch with him. "They don't make TV shows like this anymore, son," he said. Jake had been inclined to agree. Amidst all the memories, he remembered one of his favorite Gilligan episodes called "Wrongway Feldman." Now that Jake thought about it, the character of Wrongway Feldman had probably been inspired by the true story of Wrong Way Corrigan.

Wrongway Feldman had been living in seclusion on the island when Gilligan discovered the pilot's plane. The castaways decided to repair the old plane but kept finding their repairs sabotaged the next day. Come to find out, it had been Wrongway Feldman sabotaging his own plane, not wanting to leave the island paradise. Since they could not persuade Wrongway to fly for help, Feldman began teaching Gilligan to pilot the plane himself. Just before Gilligan was to make his flight, Wrongway took his place out of fear Gilligan was not ready to fly. Of course, the castaways were once again not rescued.

Jake had often identified with the castaways throughout his childhood. Feeling trapped on a deserted island called his home life, he never felt rescue was even a remote possibility. Try as he might, Jake could not see a way off his island. The more he tried to figure a way off, the more discouraged he became. Running away was not an option for an 8-year-old. Where would he run? Moving out was not an option for his 10-year-old self. Where would he go? He was not old enough to work. Had no concept of how to provide for himself. Yet, it had not kept him from dreaming of the possibility. Just like for Gilligan and the other castaways, each dream and possibility always proved an exercise in futility.

Max had told him he would help him untangle the mess of his life. Maybe, just maybe, Max could help him find the way off his island. It occurred to him that Wrongway Feldman had not wanted to leave his island. In fact, during the show, Feldman had actually made it back to civilization, found it nothing like he had hoped for, and flown back! Jake often wondered if this could be true—that maybe things weren't any better anywhere else. But what he began to experience by spending time at the Jones home told him there just might be hope of escape after all.

Jake was taken aback by how Max treated his wife and children. Whenever Mr. Jones had Livy do something around the house, he simply asked. No yelling or demanding! Livy's three little brothers, ages 8, 10, and 12, respectively, were rambunctious, disorderly, and mischievous, but never seemed to rile Max Jones! The very moment he'd fallen apart in Max's arms, the boys had been wrestling in the living room. During the scuffle, they had inadvertently knocked a lamp from a table next to the couch, causing it to shatter into pieces. Excusing themselves, Max and Linda had gone to the other room. Jake overheard everything.

"Boys! What's going on in here?" Max asked sternly.

"We were wrestling, dad. It's my fault," replied the oldest boy, Jimmy.

"It took more than one to wrestle, Jim," replied Max. "What have I told you boys about wrestling in the house?"

"Here it comes," Jake recalled thinking, "the real man will come out in anger"

"Dad, it really was my fault," continued Jimmy. "I

knew better...the rules. Will you forgive me for not taking it outside? I'm the oldest. I should have been a better brother to Rod and Ty."

And while Jake waited for Mr. Jones to fly into an uncontrolled rage at the boy's confession, what happened next stunned him.

"Yes, I forgive you," replied Max. "That was your mother's favorite lamp, son. You need to talk with her."

Jimmy, with more maturity than most men Jake had encountered and more than Jake—spoke to his mother. "Mom, it really was my fault the lamp broke. Will you forgive me?"

"Of course, I forgive you, son," replied Linda as she began picking up the pieces from the floor.

"No, hon. They made the mess. They need to clean it up. And boys," Max continued, "I expect you all to chip in an equal share in buying your mother a new lamp. You can work it off with extra chores around the house."

"Yes, sir," came the simultaneous reply.

That moment had stuck with Jake through the years. At first, he thought it too good to be true, that Max Jones was putting on a show because he wanted something from Jake in return. After all, that was reality to him. But what Jake experienced in living life knowing the Jones family proved to be the farthest thing from his reality. Even though he expected Max to lose it, he never did. He proved himself to be a man of his word. A man of honor. And Jake ate it all up.

When Max spoke to Linda, his tone echoed with

sincere admiration and respect for her, like she had value beyond what she could do for him! In fact, from that day in the kitchen, Jake had been privileged to see what he came to call "real manliness" lived out in front of him. Max Jones seemed to relish serving his wife and children! Like they were his life. Like they were worth his time and effort. Like he thought more of them than he thought of himself.

In time, Livy's brothers came to be like brothers to him and treated him like Max treated him. Jake thought of them as mini-versions of Max. Sure, they had their moments of boyish selfishness, but always seemed to be able to overcome those moments. At first, he was taken aback by this most unexpected treatment. He assumed that once they found out what he was really like, they would treat him as he had come to expect to be treated. But that never happened.

The universe seemed to have given him a parachute after all. From that day in the kitchen, Jake's life had never been the same. He was full of hope. It was like he had not only been granted a way off the desert island of life, but also that he might just learn to fly himself. He longed for moments with the Jones family. He made excuses for just happening to walk by their home. Whenever Owen would send him to the store, Jake would go considerably out of his way to the market near the Jones residence. More often than not, some member of the Jones family would stick their head out the front door as he traipsed by, having come to expect to see him. In fact, Jake began to spend more and more time at the Jones home, making excuses to his own dad and mom. He should have known better, but the feeling he had with the Jones family always overrode the fear he experienced in his own. He soon grew accustomed to the tug-of-war with his dad.

"Dad, I'm gonna go over to spend some time with the Jones boys," seventeen-year-old Jake said innocently enough so as to not elicit a negative response from Owen. "The hell you are!" yelled Owen. "You have chores to do here!"

"But, dad, I mowed the yard. I took out the trash. I loaded the dishwasher. I even cleaned my room, and mom says she's fine with me going over there."

"Your mom's not the boss, boy! You'll do what I say! There's plenty more that needs to be done around here, like...uh...er...well...just get your lazy butt to work! I don't want to hear anymore about the Jones boys!"

Each afternoon was the same. Jake's dad would forbid him from going to the Jones house. And each time, Jake's mom would take her son aside and say, "Give him a few minutes, son. As soon as he is asleep, just go and enjoy yourself. He'll never remember the conversation anyway."

Colette Owens just wanted to protect her son. Seeing the twinkle in Jake's eye each time he spoke of Max Jones or a member of the Jones family gave her a kind of joy that only a mother could feel. A mother trapped in a loveless, abusive marriage and saw no way out for herself, but was determined to help her son escape. Colette was jealous of the Jones family at first.

But the more she saw those faint hints of joy gleaming in her boy's eyes, the more the jealousy gave way to thankfulness. Although she could not even fathom a family like the Jones family being a reality, she saw the evidence and hoped her son would be helped rather than hurt for a change.

On one of those days when Jake just happened to walk by, Max and Linda were on the front porch, swaying in the old-fashioned porch swing. They had not seen Jake walk up behind them. Had not realized, until it was too late, that Jake had overheard their conversation.

In a split second, Jake's new world—his acceptance into a "loving" family—was shattered. What happened next reminded him of Wrongway Feldman, sabotaging his own escape. At that same moment, the sudden lurching of the plane he was on, careening to the ground, brought him back to the present.

11

SELF-SABOTAGE

> There are seeds of self-destruction in all of us that will bear only unhappiness if allowed to grow.
>
> DOROTHEA BRANDE

Amidst the nagging aroma of that steak and baked potato, the plane lurched and Jake's thoughts returned to something Michael said following his outburst about the lack of response on the part of the other passengers to their collective reality.

"What would Livy say? What would she do if she were here right now? Listen, Jake. What would she say?"

Turning to Michael again, Jake asked, "How do you know my wife's name? I never mentioned her name to you. Who are you?"

"Now is not the time to be asking that question. It

will be answered soon enough," came Michael's calm reply.

"Now is not the time? What is wrong with you? We are all going to die! There is no time!" yelled Jake.

Even as those words came out of his mouth, his mind was jerked back to the moment near the home of Max and Linda Jones and that overheard conversation.

"What are we gonna do with Jake?" asked Max.

"What do you mean?" asked Linda.

"Sometimes I feel a little lost as to how to help him, to be honest. His family life is pretty messed up, Linda," said Max.

"He just needs to be loved, dear," replied Linda.

"I know...but..." replied Max.

"But what?" asked Linda.

"But I don't want to sacrifice our own

children or our time with them," said Max. "Are we helping our children by exposing them to Jake?"

"Of course we are helping them, Max," said Linda. "Our children need to learn to serve others...to learn how to love even the most difficult ones to love."

"But what if he hurts one the boys? What if he hurts Livy? My first priority is to our own children...to protect them. What if Jake never learns to deal with his anger?"

That was enough for Jake. He had been right all along. He should have listened to that little voice in his head telling him to be cautious about the Jones family, that they were really no different than any other family, that this was all too good to be true. Jake ran all the way home without stopping. He hadn't even noticed that, in his haste to get away, he had run right through the pile of leaves the Jones boys had raked into a mound that very morning. He didn't know that Max and Linda had seen him running away. He never saw the look of dismay or heard them gasp, "Oh, no!" He didn't hear them calling out for him to stop or see Max running after him.

He remembered running into his house without saying a word. Like viewing his past on a massive drive-in movie screen, he relived that moment. He remembered feeling that his destructive home was a sanctuary. The irony of that feeling! That something that only brought him pain and sorrow and suffering could be his refuge! And then he remembered how foolish it had been to believe that such a thing could even be possible! His only conclusion? Hopelessness. Utter hopelessness.

With his head buried in his pillow, Jake didn't hear the knock at the front door. But he remembered the unfamiliar steps coming down the hallway toward his door. They were too firm and steady for his mom to have made and too unwavering to be those of his dad. As he lay there wondering whom these strange steps could possibly belong to, his tears were interrupted by a firm knock, knock, knock on his door.

"Jake. Jake, it's Max. Can I come in?"

Snidely, Jake replied, "I didn't think you wanted to be around someone so hurtful. Just go away!"

"Jake, come on. Let me in. I can explain," pled Max.

"There's nothing to explain," said Jake. "I heard you loud and clear. Please, just go away."

And then he heard an all-too-familiar voice. "What's going on here?" asked Owen Owens.

"Mr. Owens, I'm Max Jones...a friend of Jake's. I'm afraid I've hurt your son—offended him. I'm just trying to make things right."

"What do you mean, you've hurt my son?" asked Owen.

"I said some things—he overheard some things—I never intended for him to hear...never intended to be hurtful. I'd really like to just say my piece, Mr. Owens, and then I'll get out of your hair."

"He's not worth the effort. He'll just ignore you anyway. Do what he wants. Hell, he doesn't even give me the time of day," retorted the obviously inebriated Owen. "Go ahead. Say what you need to say. You'll see. Waste of time, if you ask me."

Jake felt thrown under the bus, as usual, by his dad. He was embarrassed to have Max Jones in his home. The home that had fallen into disrepair due to his dad's alcoholism. The home his mother tried to keep up as best she could in spite of the constant verbal and emotional abuse but that was not as clean and fresh and up-to-date as the Jones home. The home that was embarrassingly dark and smelly and as unkempt as Jake's mind felt most of the time. He felt humiliated.

"Jake, let me in. I'd really like to have a word with you. I promise...it won't take long."

Nothing.

"Jake. Please let me in."

Nothing.

After a few moments of no response, Max said, "Jake, I'm gonna stay here until you let me in so you might as well let me in."

"Please," sobbed Jake. "Just go away!"

"Ha! Ha! Ha! Ha!" laughed Owen. "I told you! Not worth your time or effort."

Turning to Owen Owens, Max gently replied, "Mr. Owens, I beg to differ with you. Jake is worth any time or any effort needed to repair our relationship. Now, I will honor you if you ask me to leave, but I cannot agree with you concerning your son being worthless. Quite the contrary. The Jake I know—the Jake I have wounded—is absolutely worth it."

"Well! Well! Well!" replied Owen. "Do tell! What kind of kiss-ass man are you that you've got to kowtow to a sissified little peckerwood?"

"Please, Mr. Owens. Just let me try. I can't expect you to understand. But as one man to another—one dad to another—what if he is all you say he is? So, what? Doesn't every boy deserve at least the respect we ourselves would hope to receive from someone else?"

As if suddenly shocked into a moment of lucidity by the question, Owen Owens simply replied, "I don't deserve respect. Why should my boy?"

"Mr. Owens, I respect you as the man of this house. I respect you as the husband of Jake's mom, and I respect you as Jake's dad. I respect you enough to ask you this: If you could give your son the things you never had, would you?"

Jake recalled the silence his dad was reduced to in

that moment. Even from his bed where he still lay with his face in his pillow, like thunder echoing so loud it drowned out the constant drone of the wind outside the plane, the lack of response on his dad's part spoke volumes. Like words longed for but never expected to be heard, Jake's dad said though slurred speech, "Yes...I would love to give my son all the things I never had...but...I'll never be able to." Owen slid down to a sitting position on the floor, leaned his back against the damp wall and began to sob. While Max Jones knelt down to comfort Owen, Jake cracked the door and peered out into the dark hallway.

He saw and heard the whole thing. As he had done for Jake in the Jones kitchen that day, Max was now doing the same thing for his dad.

Comfort. One man baring unspoken agony, spewing out of the depths of his anguished soul from some long-ago-buried pain. Jake stood there frozen. In shock at his father's vulnerability. As if witnessing a violent car crash and the subsequent triage to the victim, he listened as Max Jones became EMT to Owen Owens.

Sitting down beside Owen, Max put his arm around him. In words full of masculine strength yet clothed in tenderness, Max asked, "What is it, Mr. Owens?"

"I've tried and tried to do what's best for my boy. My boys...but ever since...ever since..." sobbed Owen.

"Ever since what?" asked Max.

"Ever since Jared..." moaned Jake's dad.

"Who is Jared?" asked Max.

"He was my son! I couldn't save him! I tried! I really

tried...but...but...he was just gone! And it was my fault...all my fault!" wailed Owen.

Gently cradling Jake's dad and rocking ever so slightly back and forth, Max said, "Tell me about Jared."

While Jake watched unnoticed from the doorway, Owen poured out his drunken soul to Max. "He was only 5 years old! He was my pride and joy! We had gone to the park that day...I had promised him I would teach him how to fish. I turned my back just for a few seconds...I promise...it was no more than a few seconds. But when I turned around, he was just gone!"

Owen began to sob uncontrollably again. Max held him in that masculine around-the-shoulder bear hug, put his head against Owen's head and began to cry with him! Jake did not know what to do. Stunned and paralyzed, he listened.

After a couple of minutes, Owen unleashed years and years of pain. Like a rippling earthquake, he went on.

"He had fallen into the water and hit his head on a rock...the water wasn't even that deep...but the rock...I tried to tell myself 'at least he hadn't suffered'...but he'd still be here if I had been half a dad!"

Squeezing Owen tightly, Max said, "I'm so sorry, Owen. I'm so sorry." More sobbing. More wailing. More pouring out.

"I got him out of the water! I tried to help him breathe, but he was just...gone. One minute, he was there...laughing and smiling...so proud of himself, standing there holding that little fishing pole. And the next he was gone. Why did I have to turn away? I was just getting a bobber out of the tackle box! I mean, I literally just turned around for a few seconds."

More sobbing. More holding.

"I couldn't even say anything at the service...too embarrassed! What kind of dad lets his boy die like that?"

While Jake watched, all he could think was, "Is this real or am I dreaming? Is this hard, callous-hearted Owen Owens or has some impostor invaded dad's body?" And then, like an airplane crashing and burning, he began to relive the moment he had first hated Jared.

12

HATE AND PAIN

> Darkness cannot drive out darkness; only light can do that. Hate cannot drive out hate; only love can do that.
>
> MARTIN LUTHER KING, JR.

> The weak can never forgive. Forgiveness is the attribute of the strong.
>
> MAHATMA GANDHI

Although falling through the air with hundreds of other people, Jake still felt alone. Alone in his thoughts. Alone in his feelings. Alone in a crowd. Nothing new for him. He had grown accustomed to that feeling. There is something about loneliness that he actually welcomed, but at least in his loneliness no one could hurt him. But even that realization hurt! That's what caused him to welcome his dad's painful barbs and insults back in the day. At least he was talking to him. How could he be in such fear yet still think about what that steak and baked potato might taste like? Loneliness mingled with the aroma of a long-anticipated meal—with a strong dose of bitterness to boot!

Jake was born a year after Jared died. A replacement baby. A surprise. In fact, his dad often referred to him as "Oops Owens" when talking with others about him. Jake figured out soon enough that he had actually been an accident. A mistake. Not wanted in the first place. While he pondered such things, he heard his dad's voice.

"Jared! Jared!" cried Owen Owens. He started drinking again after Jared died. Most nights ended the same way in the Owens home. When he was able to hold down a job, he would come home and drown his sorrows. Jake had never known anything different. Since his earliest recollections, all he had heard was how wonderful Jared had been. How terrible it had been to lose him. Owen always seemed to measure Jake according to his memories of Jared.

"Jared was a happy kid. Why can't you smile more, boy?

"Jared was a little jokester...and he could take a joke, too. Lighten up, boy.

"Jared used to help me with the car, had a little plastic tool set. Why, that little stinker would pretend to help me tune the carburetor... help me change the tire. He was always right at my feet. Why don't you do that, boy?

"Why can't you be more like Jared? More like Jared...more like Jared..." the words echoed.

He had never known Jared, but he had grown to hate him. Hated the comparisons. Hated the memory of the one who he could never live up to. Hated the shrine—the grouping of pictures his mom had placed on the mantle. Constant reminders of how far short of the glory of Jared he had fallen. Hated his brother.

Jake never mentioned the fact that he had a brother. Even when asked. This had been one small way he could control a portion of his own life. A safe haven away from the constant reminder of how unworthy he was to walk the same ground the amazing Jared had walked.

Then the voice of Max Jones broke the downward spiral of thought. With the sudden jerk of the screeching jet, Jake's thoughts transported him back to his dad's encounter with Livy's dad. Now he was back at home with Max and Owen.

"Jake, you never told me you had a brother," said Max.

"He doesn't even acknowledge his own brother. Never has," sobbed Owen, still crumpled on the floor.

"Why would you not want me to know about your brother?" asked Max.

Hemming and hawing, Jake spoke hesitantly. "It just...it just...it just hurts too much."

"I'm so sorry, Jake. So sorry, Owen. Tell me about your boy," said Max.

"He was the best," began Owen. "He was so bright. So fun to be with. So good...but..."

"But what?" urged Owen.

"But...I let him down. Why did I have to turn away? I let him down! And my dad...my dad..." whimpered Owen like a little boy.

Seeing his dad like that frightened Jake. He'd seen his dad pretty messed up, but never losing it like this!

"Your dad what?" implored Max. "Tell me, Owen. It'll be okay."

"He blamed me for the loss of his grandson! At the funeral...at the *funeral*... he had the nerve to say, 'What kind of father are you?' In front of God and everyone! My own dad! Made me feel like a loser. Like a nothing. At my own boy's funeral! What an asshole!"

Max just held Owen and turned his gaze toward Jake, saying with his eyes, "I understand, son...and I'm so sorry."

And then Owen said the strangest thing. "My dad never even told me he loved me! Not once! Never! Not even when I was a boy. Not... once..."

With that revelation, Jake suddenly understood how his dad had arrived at this place of utter devastation and why he had never told Jake he loved him. Not once. Never. Jake remembered it all as the plane descended ever closer to the ground. Now he knew why his dad could not possibly have given him something he had never been given in his own life. Still, Jake felt his dad should have been able to at least be kind to him, that somewhere deep inside he must have had an inkling of how to treat another human being! He still hated Jared and despised his father.

Again, Jake's thoughts were interrupted by a Max Jones memory.

"Jake, I need to ask you something."

Taken by surprise at this statement, Jake had not responded. How out of place. How odd. It was the first time Jake Owens had ever been asked for someone's forgiveness. The first time he had ever seen forgiveness sought in such a humble manner...and by a man!

"Jake," said Max. "Jake."

"Yeah?" Jake answered feebly.

"I need you to forgive me. I mean I need to ask you for your forgiveness."

"Huh?" replied Jake.

"I was wrong," said Max, matter-of-factly.

"Wrong? About what?"

"About the things I said—the things you overheard me say—back on my porch. The things I said that made you run away," said Max softly.

Bowing up in pride, Jake spewed, "Oh, you mean the line about how difficult I am? Or the line about how I'm a danger to your precious kids?"

"Yeah. That," replied the humbled Max.

"Jake, I was wrong to say you were a possible danger to my children...to my family. Truth is, I would die for any one of them if it meant they might live. One of the ways I do that is with my time. My children need my time. When I take time away from them to help someone else, I have to be...I need to be... careful. Careful that my own children do not feel neglected by even my best intentions toward another. They and my wife are my first priority. Always. And that will never change. That is all I was trying to communicate...but..."

"Here it comes. 'But.' There's always a but..." Jake's voice trailed off in discouragement.

"But I could have said it more clearly. Jake, the absolute truth is...we...my family...I love you, son."

"Oh, I get it. I'm your family project now, huh? You goody-two-shoes are all alike! All I am is some weird notch on your do-gooder belt!" hissed Jake. "I'm nobody's project! Can't you see? This is just the way it is! This is just the way I am! This is just reality!"

Max waited for Jake to get it all out. Encouraged him to. "Let it out, son. Let it all out."

And let it out he did!

"I can't do this anymore! I just can't! I might as well be dead. Everyone would be better off without me! Besides, I don't even exist as far as he's concerned," said Jake, pointing at Owen.

"He doesn't give a crap about me beyond what I can do for him! Hell, I was never wanted in the first place! Am I right, Owen? Dad? Tell him! Tell Max about me being your little accident! Go on! Tell him! And while you're at it, tell him what you call me. Oops Owens! Oops Owens! Oh, and my favorite. I'm your little peckerwood! Tell him, dad! Just tell him! Tell him how I, in no way, shape, or form have ever even come close to measuring up to precious little dead Jared! I HATE JARED!"

"Enough!" shouted Owen. "Enough."

Shocked at the sudden change in Owen Owens, both

Jake and Max became instantly quiet, like they'd seen an unexpected bolt of lightning.

"Jake...son. You're right. You never measured up. You never got my love. I've been so blind...so...wrong."

Stunned, Jake just stood there, door fully open now, watching the two grown men sitting on the floor, embracing each other awkwardly around the shoulders.

"You're right, son. I never even told you I...I never told you how much...I...I...love you."

Silence. And then, as if suddenly and miraculously sober, Owen Owens began to speak.

"I...I...love you, son. My dad never told me, so I didn't even know how to tell you, but that's no excuse. There is no excuse. Seems I've hidden for far too long inside my head...and I've ruined everything in the process. I ruined your mother. I ruined the memory of Jared. And I ruined you. Son...my son.... Jake...my precious boy...I've been so wrong. Will you...could you...forgive me...?"

Jake didn't know what to do or say. Having absolutely no frame of reference for such a moment, he froze. Then Max was standing next to him, one arm around his shoulders while his other arm lifted Owen from the floor, bringing father and son together.

"Your father asked you a question, Jake," said Max

Bursting into tears and falling into his father's arms, all Jake could say was "Yes! Yes! Yes! Yes! Yes! Yes! Yes," in what felt like the safest place on Earth. While the two men held on tight in an endless bear hug of reconciliation, Colette, having anxiously overheard the entire exchange, rushed into the fray and found a bit of redemption for herself and her family.

As Max excused himself, he whispered into Jake's ear, "Forgiveness sure looks good on you, son."

Although things continued to be difficult between he and his dad even after that day, they were never the same. The family—he had a real family—began to experience real, honest relationship. Real, honest healing. Real, honest grief over the loss of Jared. Real, life-giving honesty.

Jake remembered looking at himself in the mirror after that moment just as he had done in the plane's lavatory early on in the flight, and saying, "Forgiveness *does* looks good on you."

13

IN FLIGHT

We are continually shaped by the forces of coincidence.

PAUL AUSTER

Without warning, Jake again felt a stark panic, which now began to rise from the other passengers in the plane. With the first wave of shock wearing away, the whimpers grew into cries. The cries grew into wails. The wails gave way to screams of terror. Prayers could be heard going up all around. Even the atheists on board suddenly found religion, crying out into the cathedral the Trantex airliner had become. And then his eyes met the eyes of Michael and locked there.

Still appalled that Michael was not reacting to what should have sent him into a raving panic like everyone else, Jake was at once incredulous and confused. Michael's non-response continued to bewilder and anger him. Why it bothered him so much, he did not know. It just did. But then he had one of those moments one has when seeing a long forgotten face—an epiphany of sorts. "I've seen you before!" Jake said out loud.

Michael locked onto Jake's stare, which only freaked Jake out more, causing his eyes to grow as wide as saucers. "Yes! I've seen you before! I *know* it!"

"We've never met, Jake. Not really," Michael replied.

"Wait...what?" replied Jake. "We've never met...not really? That means we *have* met! I knew it!"

Jake couldn't put his finger on it. He had not noticed it when he had first met Michael, but in his mind—in this moment—he knew he'd seen him before. As the jet continued its rapid descent, Jake once again plunged into the depths of his mind to places long forgotten. Just as he had done when preparing for this flight, he remembered happening upon a website listing famous people who had perished in plane crashes. Perhaps it was morbid curiosity, but mostly it was because he felt he "knew" many of those who had died due to their indelible etching into his mind.

Of course, there were people like Amelia Earhart, the famous female flyer who had been the first woman to fly solo across the Atlantic. What made her so significant in his mind was the fact that during her famous attempt to circumnavigate the world in 1937, she had disappeared somewhere over—in—the Pacific Ocean. He had been fascinated with her story since he had seen that first short documentary as a boy. Why he was thinking of her now, he had no idea. Yet, there was something about her story that caused him to think of Michael! Weird.

Just as he strained to answer the question of how Amelia Earhart had reminded him of Michael, he heard in, his mind, John Denver singing "Rocky Mountain High." His dad loved John Denver. Some of Jake's favorite boyhood memories—actual moments of peace—came whenever a John Denver song, especially "You Fill Up My Senses," drifted from the radio he kept playing in the garage. Often, Owen would shush Jake and say, "Listen, boy. Just listen...his music just does something to my soul." During those brief songs, Jake felt like he had been given a three-minute oasis of peace in which he could catch his breath.

He remembered the day he heard the news. He was sweeping the garage while his dad drunkenly fiddled with the engine of the family car. With the strains of "Calypso" weaving their way beneath the words of the news announcer, he watched his dad bury his head in his hands in silent despair—as if he had just heard that his best friend had been killed. John Denver, while flying an experimental aircraft near Pacific Grove, California, had crashed into Monterey Bay. Although he could not have known at the time, there now seemed to be some connection to John Denver and Michael. Again, weird.

Before he could even consider what that connection might be, Jake suddenly remembered another of his dad's favorites, actor Audie Murphy. As a boy, he had often watched the real World War II hero heroically save the day in movies like "To Hell and Back," "Destry," and "The Cimarron Kid" while his dad snored away in his recliner. How he dreamed what life would have been like had Audie Murphy been his dad! How he daydreamed of riding alongside Audie in those old reruns of spaghetti westerns. Audie, along with four others, had perished when the Aero Commander they were riding in crashed into a Virginia mountainside during a heavy thunderstorm. And Jake thought...of Michael.

And there were others. Memories of news reels past and Fox News reports more recently. Like that day in July of 1999. Jake, then only eleven years old, had heard of the Kennedys his whole life. He'd even seen the old footage when John Jr. had saluted his father's casket as it passed by in procession in the nation's capital in 1963. Now, he remembered the shock he felt when he heard that John Kennedy Jr. had been killed, along with his wife and her sister, in a plane crash off the coast of Martha's Vineyard, Massachusetts. He could not see for the life of him how or why that event would make him think of Michael, but it did.

Then, later that year, golfer Payne Stewart and others in his party died when the private jet they were flying in inexplicably lost pressurization. They were all dead before they hit the ground. But why did it make him think of his seatmate?

Before he could make the connection between these crashes and Michael, he thought of September 11, 2001. He remembered watching Fox News—his dad often watched it in the morning after breakfast—and seeing the planes crash into the World Trade Center in New York City. The anchor broke the news of another plane, American Airlines flight 77, slamming into the Pentagon and later announced that one of their own, commentator Barbara Olsen, had been on Flight 77. And he thought of Michael.

As he had experienced with the music of John Denver, the wordless orchestral music of James Horner began to fill his mind with the familiar themes of "Braveheart," "Legends of the Fall," and "Titanic." He used to listen to those very soundtracks for hours upon end, allowing their beautiful melodies and lush orchestrations to inspire his own creativity. And how he had mourned when he heard the news of Horner's death in June of 2015. The famous film composer and Jake's personal favorite had crashed near Santa Barbara while piloting his own plane. And this made him think of Michael.

Now images and footage from the news reports played back in his mind. The search for Amelia Earhart. Navy and private vessels alike combed the ocean for any sign of her or her plane. He saw blurred faces of crewmembers on search planes. Faces. Faces. And then just one face.

Michael.

Jake could see the face of the one he now stared at as if he was seeing a ghost! On the search plane, in the old scratchy footage, he was sure of it. Michael had been there. So briefly. Like a holographic image that toggles between clarity and indistinguishable pixels, the longer Jake gazed into that face, the more he realized it could only be Michael!

Once again, before he could process this revelation, he saw old newspaper images of the crew searching Monterey Bay for the wreckage of John Denver's crashed plane. Sure enough, there on one of the small Coast Guard vessels, wearing a ball cap, stood Michael!

He saw that newspaper clipping of the wreckage of Audie Murphy's plane in Virginia. There, scouring the crash site, digging through debris, was Michael!

He recognized Michael's face in the memories from the Kennedy crash, the Payne Stewart crash, and the Pentagon crash. There was no doubt! Michael had been in each and every one of those pictures and brief shots of film footage! Now he stared directly into those familiar eyes, and they stared back at him with calm, with no fear, with a knowing.

"How...?"

Michael continued to stare into Jake's bewildered eyes. Waiting for something more.

"How is that—how is *this*—even possible?" asked Jake.

"We don't have much time, Jake. I cannot answer all your questions, but I will answer the necessary ones," replied Michael.

"Just...how?" said Jake.

Before Michael could answer, Jake asked, "Who *are* you?"

"That's a better question, Jake. That's one I can

answer," Michael replied. "I was sent to you for such a time as this," he began.

"Such a time as this? My death! Are you kidding me? What kind of kook are you?" shouted Jake.

"I wasn't sent for this one trip with you, Jake. I was sent the moment you were conceived. I've been with you the whole time."

"I must be losing it now!" shouted Jake. "This is real, Michael...the plane...we're going to die...come on! Stop messing with my head!"

"Yes, you are going to die. That is inevitable, but I am sent to go through *with* you. I am sent with a word of comfort for you... as a sign."

Breathless and freaking out, Jake did not even have a response to Michael's lunacy.

"Oh, right! Someone *sent* you? Are you God or something? Who do you think you are?!"

"No, I am not God...but it is He who sent me," replied Michael.

"You've got to be freaking kidding me!" yelled Jake.

Michael just sat there, staring intently into Jake's darting eyes.

After what seemed like an eternity of awkwardness —at least on Jake's part—a thought occurred to him.

"If God sent you, tell me something no one else could possibly know!"

Not missing a beat, Michael replied, "From the time you were a boy and even until you graduated from college, you never put your hands in your pockets like other boys did because you did not feel you deserved to be seen as a real boy, a real man. You thought yourself less than a boy. Less than a real man. And placing your hands in your pockets would have been a lie."

Jake stared deeply into Michael's eyes, wanting more.

Speaking softly, almost as if to himself, Jake said, "I've never told *anyone*. How...?"

"And there's one more thing," replied Michael. "I can tell you the very moment that all changed."

14

EPIPHANY

> Godly sorrow is a gift of the Spirit. It is a deep realization that our actions have offended our Father and our God. It is the sharp and keen awareness that our behavior caused the Savior, He who knew no sin, even the greatest of all, to endure agony and suffering.
>
> EZRA TAFT BENSON

> It makes no difference how deeply seated may be the trouble, how hopeless the outlook, how muddled the tangle, how great the mistake. A sufficient realization of love will dissolve it all.
>
> EMMET FOX

While Jake sat there with his mouth gaping wide, Michael continued. "Remember..." He touched the side of Jake's head.

Instantly, Jake was transported back to the moment when Max Jones finished what he started the day that Owen had sought Jake's forgiveness. Because of all that transpired so unexpectedly there outside Jake's bedroom door, Max had felt it best to wait for another time to seek Jake's forgiveness for himself. A few days after that momentous event in the brief history of Jake Owens, he was in the Jones' kitchen once again. Looking back, he found it kind of humorous and profound that so much food for the soul had been served up and received in that place.

After a few minutes of small talk, Max addressed the elephant in the room. Somehow, Jake knew it had to be done. That something unfinished had been drawing him to this moment. "Jake, remember the question I asked you back at your house?"

Jake nodded, casting his eyes to the floor.

"Jake, I was wrong to have spoken about you the way I did that day. You are *not* a danger to my family. You are *not* just some project I am working on. I am *not* trying to fix you, son. The truth is just as much as you think you need us, we need you. Just as much as you feel you are a project in need of attention, I am a project—a work in progress myself. Just as much as you feel you need to be fixed, I have broken places in my own life in need of repair. That being said, Jake, I need to ask you again. I was wrong. Will you forgive me?"

Without hesitation, Jake got up from the barstool where he had been leaning and wrapped his arms around Max.

"I forgive you, Max." And the tears began to flow again. This time, though, they were not tears of sorrow, but tears of release and acceptance and affirmation and joy. Sheer, uninhibited, rarely experienced joy of the human soul as only expressed in the depths of relationship. One exchanging life with another.

After a few moments of pure peace, Jake felt a new freedom. Something he could not recall having felt before. Yet, for all the freshness and freedom he felt in that moment, there were things that continued to nag at his soul. The honesty, rather than a thing to be feared, had actually brought about a new capacity to feel. To feel something rather than numbness. Even in that moment of clarity and renewal of emotional capacity, he could feel a deeper burden. A deeper longing. Then it dawned on him. Before he could catch himself, Jake blurted out, "What do you mean you have broken places in your life? How are you anyone's work in progress?"

"Jake, there are some things you need to know about me. Let's sit down."

As the two men shuffled to the kitchen table and sat down, Jake said, "Mr. Jones... Max...your life is perfect. I mean, look. You have an awesome wife and four awesome kids. You have a great job. Everyone loves you."

Chuckling, Max said, "It hasn't always been this way, Jake. There was a time when you might say Max Jones was bad news."

"Get out of here!" laughed Jake. "No way do I believe that!" Max grew serious and silent, and Jake felt a sudden reverence for this man he respected so much. As if he were about to be given a rich secret, a treasure, from the heart of one man to another.

"Jake, please keep what I am about to tell you between you and me."

Nodding and fully attentive to Max's demeanor and words, Jake sat in complete anticipation of what he was about to hear.

"In many ways, my younger self—my younger life—was a lot like yours. I had an older brother who was the star athlete. The good-looking one. The big man on campus. The dreamed of and hoped for firstborn son of my dad. Marty could do no wrong in my dad's eyes, and I found myself always trying to live up to the stats of my big brother...trying to live up to my dad's expectations. Never worked for me, though. There came a point in my life where I realized I could never earn my dad's approval or shine bright enough to eclipse the glory of my brother's accomplishments. So you know what I did, Jake?"

Shaking his head "no," Jake focused on Max's every word.

"Jake, I gave up. Just plain old stopped trying. In fact, I went the opposite direction. One day I just decided that if I could not gain my dad's attention by being good, I'd do whatever felt good to ME. If my dad couldn't love me when I was being good, then what difference would it make if I did whatever the hell I wanted?"

Stopping as if to catch his breath, Max, who had

been looking directly at Jake as he had been speaking, turned his eyes downward, as if in shame. Jake took notice because something in that look was very familiar. He knew shame all too well, but for the life of him he could not understand how to deal with it. So, like many men do, he buried it under layer upon layer of emotional pain and human failure and grew more and more numb with each new layer.

"Jake...I...I fell in with a few other guys who were dealing—or NOT dealing—with similar things I was dealing with. One thing led to another. You see, I was trying to numb the pain of my dad's rejection. And I found something that really did numb me at least for a few moments in the grand scheme of things. A buddy introduced me to drugs. At first, it was just a few innocent drags on a joint. But that was all it took for me to conclude the pleasure and peace and lack of mental and emotional pain I experienced in those moments was worth the fear of being caught. It didn't take long, though, for the pain to outweigh the benefits of the weed," Max said with a slight laugh in his voice.

Jake did not laugh. He was too stunned by the revelation he was hearing from his hero!

"Jake, I went from cocaine to heroin to LSD to huffing to whatever I could get my hands on. The details are beside the point, though. By the time I realized I was addicted, it was too late. And then I got busted."

Jake was on the edge of his seat. "Busted? By the police? And then what!?"

As if gathering himself to bare a dark secret, Max

said, "Yes, by the police. I'll never forget the shame I felt. Handcuffed. Mug shot. Calling my dad..."

This time, Jake did not break the silence, but, sensing the gravity of what Max was about to share next, he simply waited out of respect.

"My dad was embarrassed. He told me I had humiliated him. Tarnished the good name of our family. His good name...and that I was no son of his."

After a few seconds so thick they could have been cut with a knife, Max continued. "He told me I had made my bed, so I needed to lie in it. He left me there in jail. Overnight. Jake, I believe that was the right thing for him to do now that I look back. He was trying to teach me personal responsibility...that my choices have consequences...but when he came to bail me out the next day, all he said was, 'You'll need to get your things when we get home. Since you cannot seem to live up to the name of Jones—since you seem to know what's best for your own life—you're on your own.'

"Jake, from there I just went completely downhill. Sleeping in the park. Crashing on friends' couches. Breaking into abandoned houses just to get out of the weather. Sleeping around."

Now, Max was getting emotional.

As this memory continued, Jake remembered the emotion of the next revelation. Like Max was in a free fall. And he had been.

"Jake, I got a girl pregnant."

Jake was stunned.

His curiosity outweighing any trepidation, he asked, "Was it Linda?"

Silence. And more silence.

Finally, shaking his head, Max said, "No. It was someone I had only slept with one time. It was bad, Jake. Her parents wanted to keep it quiet, but everyone knew. They shipped her off to stay with relatives in another state. Told me I was to never have contact with their daughter again or they'd bring rape charges against me. Jake, she was only 16 years old. I was barely 18."

Max collected his thoughts and quieted his emotions.

"I have a son. A son I've never met, Jake. A son I've never been allowed to even see from a distance. Oh, I tried to offer financial support through the years. Asked to see him. Her dad just laughed and said, 'You can't buy your way out of what you've done, boy. You should have kept it in your pants.' I just gave up after a few years, Jake. And I used to feel so guilty. Used to feel so ashamed...until..."

Jake felt he was hanging from a cliff. "Until...what?"

15

REDEMPTION

> What I absolutely want is to suggest that before it's anything else, redemption is God mending the bicycle of our souls; God bringing out the puncture repair kit, re-inflating the tires, taking off the rust, making us roadworthy once more. Not so that we can take flight into ecstasy, but so that we can do the next needful mile of our lives.
>
> FRANCIS SPUFFORD

Jake was drawn back to the present by the aroma of steak and butter-soaked baked potato! Feeling Michael's gentle hand on his face, Jake was at once appalled and intrigued by the inappropriate question Michael posed. "You gonna eat that?"

But Jake was back in the moment with Max. "Until...what?"

"Long story short, Jake, I had gotten myself into a

deep, dark pit I couldn't smoke or sleep or finagle my way out of."

"But it wasn't your fault, Max. You had no choice. Your dad...the way he treated you. The girl you got pregnant...her family...the way they treated you. The drugs...everything. You had no choice..." said Jake, empathizing completely with everything Max had just told him.

"Jake, we always have a choice."

"I had no choice in the way my life has gone," replied Jake.

"Jake, you've always had a choice, son."

Seeing the confusion on Jake's face, Max went on. "Let me finish. After a few years of stumbling around on my own, strung out on drugs, in and out of jail, I found myself living in my car and watching life pass me right by. I saw people my age living successful lives. I heard about some of my old running buddies from my teen years that had straightened out their lives, and it made me so angry. I was not a happy man, not someone anyone in their right mind would ever want to be around.

"But finally, one day, out of sheer desperation, I decided to look up one of those old friends. I heard he was running a construction company so I decided to go find him. Went to a work site where I knew he would probably be to ask him for a job. At least that's what I would say. What I was really after was to find out how he'd broken out of the old life.

"I must have looked a mess, because when I walked

up he didn't even recognize me at first. There I was in jeans that I'd probably never washed. Jake, I used to just sleep in the same clothes I wore every day. I literally had nothing except the clothes on my back and an old beat up Chevy that I could barely keep gas in.

I was mortified when he looked at me and said, "Can I help you, sir?"

"Dave! It's me! Max. Max Jones!"

"There was no way for him to hide the utter shock that came across his face, but he gathered himself enough to try and put me at ease. 'Max! Max Jones! How are you, buddy?'

"The next thing I knew, we were sitting in his work trailer on the job site. I asked him if he had any work for me. He told me he'd find something for me to do, but he didn't leave it there. You know what he said to me next, Jake? What he did?"

"No," said Jake.

"He said, 'Max, you know me well enough to know I'll shoot straight with you. You need more than a job I might be able to help you with. You need answers. Am I right?'

"Having not expected the conversation to go that direction, expecting to do as I'd always done...talk or perform my way out of tight situations...I tried to change the subject. But Dave—thank God—wouldn't let me."

"Max, I don't have time for your bullshit...and neither do you. Are you ready to stop running, brother?"

"I'm not running from anyone!"

"Max, you can't talk your way out of this life. You can't perform your way out of trouble. Just look at yourself and be honest. How is the crap you front with working out for you?"

"To be honest, Jake, I wanted to punch his lights out. I even stood and pulled back my fist. He just stood and did the most loving and brave thing. He jutted his face out and said, 'Go ahead! Hit me! If it'll make you feel better about yourself, just hit me!'

"I'll be honest with you. His balls were bigger than mine that day, thank God! In shame...that's all you could call it...I dropped my fist and headed for the door. And Dave said, 'Go ahead! Run away again, Max! But ask yourself this question: Just where are you running to?'

"And then he said something that literally changed my life: 'Max, I don't know how to help you, but I know the answer.'

"I remember stopping dead in my tracks, hand on the door knob, ready to run again, and having my heart melted by those words. He was right. Just where was I running? Then he asked, "What are you running from, Max? Seems to me you don't know where you're going, and you don't even see the baggage you drag everywhere with you. What you're living is not life. You're living out death. Tell me if I'm wrong, brother.'

"He had, of course, nailed my heart to the wall in a way. His honest question—his obvious love for me in spite of my bitterness—drew me to a moment in time that changed everything.

“I said, 'You don’t know how to help me, but you know the answer? What does that even mean, Dave?'

“His response? 'Max, I was right where you are. You know that. Drugs. Jail. Women. Not knowing if I’d wake up from one morning to the next. I just got tired of it all. One day, someone looked at me and asked me the same questions I just asked you...and I bit...just like you. And you know what they said to me? They said that the answer—the Answer—was Jesus.'

“Jake, when he said that name—Jesus—I almost got up and walked out. I had grown so tired of the goody-two-shoes Christians I’d run across in my life to that point saying one thing and doing another that I thought, ‘Here we go again.’ But I am so glad I didn’t.

“Dave went on. ‘Max, I honestly can only do so much for you...and I really do not know all the answers to all your questions, but I know that I was once as messed up as you...lost as you...confused as you...and Jesus invaded my life with crazy love, man. Crazy, mad love. Max, here’s what I can do. If you’ll let me, I will walk toward Jesus with you. I’ll be a sounding board for your questions. When you don’t understand something, you can take out your frustrations on me. When you need a shoulder to cry on, I’m your man. Been there. Still do that. And I can guarantee you this. When you fall down—and you will, son—I will be there. Not to kick you when you’re down. Not to say ‘I told you so’ but to pick you up. I’ll help you get back on your feet every time if you'll let me. Jesus is the Answer, son. Let's walk toward Him together.'

"Jake, I know I must sound like a crazy man to you right now," said Max, "but I walked out of my old life that day. I walked out of my old way of thinking. I walked right out of the frying pan into the fire of life that day, and I have never regretted that decision for one moment. Not one moment, Jake. And I want that same life for you."

Jake felt stunned, confused and yet, oddly, loved. No one had ever shared so deeply with him from such an honest place. No one had ever expressed the guilt and shame he could not even express to himself yet had borne for his entire short life. He remembered thinking, "Hell, what have I got to lose? I've pretty much tried everything else to numb my pain. Might as well try this Jesus crap."

Jake remembered everything. Every word. Every feeling. Every ounce of being loved. Not for what he had or had not done, but simply because he existed. Max explained sin. Missing the mark. He told the story of man's fall into sin. He explained God's remedy of forgiveness. How Jesus had been perfect—without sin—yet had been tempted in every manner just as Jake himself had been tempted!

Max explained the need for Jesus to lay down His life for the sake of Mankind. How the cross was a bridge between God and mankind. How the shedding of Christ's blood had paid the debt we could never repay, no matter how good they were. No matter how many good deeds they performed. He explained the resurrection of Jesus. How His triumph over sin and death meant mankind could experience the same thing, ...through simple faith. The size of the smallest particle would be enough to be restored to relationship with God.

Then Max shared the most incredible thing of all about simple faith in Jesus Christ. He told Jake that, by placing his faith in Jesus Christ, he could become a new creation, that all the old things like sleeping around, the drugs, the disobedience toward his mom and dad, anything and everything, was washed away and that by that simple faith all would be made brand new.

In the moment, the weight of the guilt in his short life had been more than enough to break him. "Max, I feel so guilty. So ashamed. I've done too much to be forgiven."

Max wisely said, "You don't get to decide the extent of God's power to forgive or whether or not He loves you, Jake. You have two choices. Either accept His love and forgiveness or reject it. That's the choice."

"But I feel so...ashamed."

"Jake, guilt is the awareness that you've done something wrong. Shame is the belief that you *are* something wrong. Jesus paid the debt for your guilt and He bore the shame you feel... on the cross...on your behalf...because you are precious to Him. Jake...you were wanted. You'd not even be here...wouldn't even exist, had He not wanted relationship with you. You are wanted."

Even though Jake did not fully understand what was

happening, He gave his heart—everything about himself—to Jesus that day. He found *the* Answer to the big question, someone to fill the abyss of hopelessness in his mind. And then it dawned on him. He did not find anything or anyone. Love had found Jake Owens.

Jake saw the question in his mind anew as the plane fell. To know and to be known. Is it possible?

While the precious aroma of that long-anticipated steak and baked potato wafted through the first class cabin, Jake again pondered Michael's question.

"You gonna eat that?"

16

LOVING AND LOSING

> Bad things do happen; how I respond to them defines my character and the quality of my life. I can choose to sit in perpetual sadness, immobilized by the gravity of my loss, or I can choose to rise from the pain and treasure the most precious gift I have—life itself.
>
> WALTER ANDERSON

Jake was weirdly amused and bemused by Michael's question: "You gonna eat that?" A question like that in a moment like this was funny yet bewildering. The sound of the plane plunging once again got his attention, but the juxtaposition of heading for certain death and the inane question brought Jake's mind to a standstill.

Again, Michael touched the side of Jake's head. Normally, Jake would have pulled away from such an action, finding the extended hand of a man toward his face too reminiscent of the many times his dad had slapped him senseless. Instantly, his memories took him back to age 13. His grandmother had died and his dad had told him, "I need to go to the funeral home to make arrangements."

Jake knew his dad was, as usual, buzzed. Before he had thought about the possible consequences, he blurted out, "I want to go with you, dad." At first, Jake told himself that someone needed to go along just to try and protect his dad. Be an extra set of clear, sober eyes on the road. Of course, Jake had an ulterior motive beyond the nobility of protecting his dad. "Wait for me, dad! I'll be right there," Jake yelled, retrieving something from his room and joining his dad in the car.

No sooner had Owen backed out of the driveway than he ran a stop sign. Jake had no time to warn his dad or see the other car headed straight for the passenger side. Luckily, the other driver saw what was about to happen and laid on the horn, causing Owen to slam on the brakes. As he did, Owen, his dad instincts miraculously kicking in, reached his arm across Jake's chest to shield him. Jake, out of fear, pushed his dad's arm away and recoiled. Owen lost it. The arm that had been extended to protect his son became a battering ram. The stack of papers and books Jake had been holding scattered to the floor.

"What the hell?" replied Owen. "What's all that crap?"

Rubbing his face to alleviate the pain that had just been inflicted on him, Jake said, "Those are the plans grandma made for her memorial service."

As if shocked into sobriety, Owen sat there dumbfounded in the middle of the intersection. "What...do you...mean?"

Tears streamed down Jake's cheeks, but he refused to be reduced to sobbing. "Grandma wanted the service to be for us...about us... rather than about her," he answered. "These are the Bible verses she wants the preacher to talk about, and these books...these songbooks...she marked songs she wanted sung."

"What songs?" asked Owen.

"Well, she wanted Amazing Grace sung for you and mom. She wanted When the Roll Is Called Up Yonder in memory...in memory of Jared. And she wanted this one...I Want to Stroll Over Heaven With You...sung...sung for...sung for...me."

They buried his grandmother and Jake went into emotional hiding. He remembered vividly his decision that day: He would never let anyone hurt him again. He would never allow himself to get close to anyone again. His relationship with grandma Owens had been, at best, distant and occasional due to her living in another city. But those rare times when he got to be with her were drops of rain in an emotional desert. Whenever she would drop by, her hands were always full of presents and such, but it was not the gifts Jake loved the most. As treasured and anticipated as those gifts were, his greatest joy was seeing her drop whatever was in her arms and reach down to embrace her "precious boy" with so much love that Jake thought he would explode with sheer ecstasy! The last time he had gotten to see her—to be hugged by her—was that way. Even at age 13, Jake melted in his grandmother's arms. Melted at the secret words she whispered into his ear: "It's gonna be okay, son. It's all gonna work out in the end. Trust me."

He could still see the gleam in her eye. That small, secret glance between a boy and his grandma that says, "I believe in you...no matter what!" He had lived on that gleam between the rare and brief visits. Had felt at least someone believed in him. At least she was there for him as much as she could be. At least he had a refuge in her. After the funeral service, he cried... sobbed...all the way to the cemetery. Standing over the casket that day, he decided to never again allow himself to be suckered in to getting close to anyone. It hurt too much when they were gone. And Jake had enough hurt in his short life.

It was soon after that decision that Jake had begun to seek comfort in the realm of his awakening sexual attractions. He had an uncanny way of spotting the girls who would be easy targets for his advances. His strategy? Find lonely girls. Look for the girls who have low opinions of themselves. Look for the girls whose daddies don't value them. Look for the girls looking for guys like him. As Jake looked back, he could see the truth. He was looking for someone exactly like himself. He was looking for someone to make him feel what he needed to feel. He needed to feel wanted...to feel known... to be loved...to know another. Someone to experience life with. He was looking for love. But all he felt was guilt and shame after every encounter—and there were many. No matter how much he told himself they wanted it, he still felt the gross feeling one gets when they have used someone for their personal gratification without regard for the needs of the one they just used.

Jake suddenly returned to the present, staring at Michael, who simply asked, "Do you remember what Livy said?"

Livy. Precious Livy. The true love of his life. And to think—in this moment of all moments—how he almost lost her.

After that day of healing he had experienced in the Jones' kitchen, Jake gave his heart—and most importantly, his mind—to Jesus. His circumstances didn't suddenly change. His dad didn't stop drinking or lashing out in anger. He still had daily battles for his thoughts. But in spite of the lack of outward change in his life and circumstances, Jake changed. On the inside. And Livy was a major reason for the change.

As if a magical spell had been cast over him that day he gave his heart to Jesus, if nothing else, his outlook on life began to change.

And with that change came the recollection of the last words his grandmother had whispered in his ear. "It's gonna be okay, son. It's all gonna work out in the end. Trust me."

It had taken Jake countless hours with Max Jones, vomiting out the questions of a dazed and confused boy trying to fight his way into manhood and basking in the deep revelation of a real man who has "been there, done that," before he faced that the way he used other people was only destroying his own soul.

Even though he had given his heart to Jesus, Jake still had occasional sexual encounters. After each release of physical energy, the bliss was quickly dispelled with utter guilt and shame, causing the encounters to lose their power over him. The more he replaced his old ways of thinking with the new ways of thinking Max was teaching him, the less he desired to hurt anyone else. And the more the old thoughts were replaced with new thoughts, the more Jake desired a real, forever relationship. As he thought about the things he would desire in such a life-long partner, he thought of things that had long-lasting value. A good sense of humor. A beautiful smile. A level head. Someone he could tell anything to without fear of being rejected. Someone who could love him in spite of his shortcomings. Someone like...Livy Jones!

Jake had grown by leaps and bounds under Max's tutelage. His mentor's words were like life to him, especially when he said, "Jake, delight yourself in the Lord and he will give you the desires of your heart."

Jake had taken those words to heart. The more he practiced talking with God, the more his point of view changed about everything. The more time he spent mulling over the truths he was learning, the more freedom he began to experience. The respect he had for Livy only intensified the more he thought about how all the qualities he could ever desire in someone else were actually embodied—personified—in Livy. So, he'd decided to pursue her!

It was innocent, his blunder. After one of those hour-long sessions with Max Jones, Jake had eaten dinner with the family. After dinner, Livy mentioned that she would like to go for a walk in the neighborhood park and asked if anyone else was up to it. No one felt like joining her, so Livy headed for the door alone.

"Where do you think you're going, young lady?" Max asked.

"Dad, I'm seventeen! I can take care of myself. I'll be fine."

Sensing his chance to be alone with Livy, Jake interjected, "I'll go with her, Mr. Jones."

"Thanks, Jake...and stop calling me Mr. Jones! It's Max!"

"Yes, sir!" Jake said as he and Livy walked out the front door.

Walking toward the park, Jake felt something he had not felt before. He believed he could be content with Livy. Be himself. He felt he loved her. Not just loved her like a brother, but IN love with her. As they walked, he could tell she felt something for him. He was walking on clouds. There was lightness in his step. An easy freedom in his words. An urging in his soul as he took her by the hand and stopped next to the swings.

Before Livy could even respond, Jake leaned in to kiss her.

His sweet reverie was broken when she pulled her hand away.

"What are you doing, Jake?"

"I'm...I...I...was...I thought..."

"You thought what, Jake?"

"I thought you...the way you talk to me... the way you look at me...the...you know!" said the exasperated boy.

"Jake, I do have feelings for you, but I value you enough to not take advantage of you. And I expect you to value me at least that much!"

Not giving Jake a chance to respond, she educated him in the value of real, life-laid-down relationship in no uncertain terms.

"Jake, if you value me...if you want a real relationship with me... you will value me. I know this sounds crazy in today's way of thinking, but if you really love me, you'll value me enough to not use me. If you truly love me, you'll get my dad's and my mom's permission to see me. If you truly value me, you will lay down your life for me. I will not waste my time with you if you do not value me enough to build a proper foundation...on faith...on Christ."

Jake felt like a scolded puppy, tempted to tuck his tail between his legs and run, but he was glad he didn't. He really did love Livy. Without realizing it early on, he had loved her since that day in the gym when she had come to his rescue.

"Well, Jake? Do you really value me for who I am or am I just another possible notch on your belt?"

Jake just looked down...for a long time. "Well?" asked Livy again.

"Livy Jones, I have never desired to protect someone like I want to protect you. I have never wanted someone as much as I want you, but it's not to use you. I'd never do that. I just want to know you...really know you. You're worth more than that to me."

"If I am really worth as much to you as you say I am, you'll lay down your life for me, Jake. I don't need you to jump through any hoops to gain my love. You already have that. I need to feel you cherish me beyond what you can get from me. I need to feel you would go through hell or high water to make me yours. I need to feel I'm worth dying for."

What Jake did next paved the way to their eventual marriage. Rather than try to talk his way into her heart, he had wisely decided to put his money where his mouth was. He walked her back home and promptly asked Max Jones for permission to pursue his daughter. From that day forward, Jake laid down his life for his Livy. He expressed her worth in the way he met all the relationship requirements her parents had placed on them. The curfews. The places they went. Never being alone without letting her parents know where they were and what their plans were. He had proven her worth time and time again, and when the time came came, she said yes. He could have lost her then, but he didn't.

As the plane careened toward Earth, he thought, "But I'm losing her now."

Then, Jake remembered something. Turning to Michael, he said, "I never mentioned Livy's name to you, Michael."

17

CHOICES

> Once I realized that right thinking is vital to victorious living, I got more serious about thinking about what I was thinking about, and choosing my thoughts carefully.
>
> JOYCE MEYER

"I know," said Michael, "but, as I've already told you, I've been with you all along. I was there the moment your life was conceived. I was even there before you were ever conceived."

"That makes absolutely no sense!" declared Jake.

"Jake, truth is this: You were in God's mind before the need for the concept of time ever existed. Before Earth and all it contains was spoken into being, you were on His mind."

Something about the way Michael said the words "you were on His mind" caused time to stand still once again. Jake's confused heart felt peace. The plane was still plummeting, passengers around him were still in full panic mode, the oxygen masks still dangled from their overhead compartments, and death was still looming, but there was no doubt about it. He felt peace.

"Jake, I am sent of God to help you make the journey."

"By 'journey' you mean...death...the final destination?" asked Jake.

"Not exactly, Jake. I've been with you each and every step of the way. What you are experiencing is simply the next step in the eternal journey. I am an angel of the Lord. My very name means 'Who Is Like God?' so that at the mention of my name mankind is reminded that there is no one who is like God. There is only One. My last name, Manzon, actually means 'messenger' and I am sent as both protector and messenger to you."

"If you've been with me all along, why am I just now seeing you?" asked Jake.

"Now is the time. There has been no need for such a revelation before this day. Though we have never met like this before, you have seen evidence of my presence. You just never had a frame of reference within which to place it or to help you understand. Jake, I am the angel of the Lord and, as such, have been given the authority to speak the Word of God to you. He has always been there. He has always loved you. He has never once left you. Never once forsaken you."

"Always been there? Never left me? Never forsaken me? How is that possible?!" demanded Jake.

Before Michael could answer, Jake went on a rant. "Where was he when I was a boy? Where was he when I had to endure all those years, all the vile sexual deviance of Old Man Winters? Where was he when my dad hit my mom? Where was he when he hit me...when he was so crazy with rage that my mom and grandma had to pull him off of me? Where was he when Happy died? Where was he when my dad was drinking away any hope for a normal family life? Where was he when I was being humiliated...shamed in front of everyone...that day in the gym? Where was he when the only person who ever seemed to give a damn for me when I was a boy...when my grandma died? Where was he, Michael? Where was he?"

Michael put his hand on Jake's shoulder. "Jake, remember the pictures? My face in the old news reels and pictures from the air crashes you researched?"

Jake nodded.

"Those were planted there—just for you—as a sign of the Truth. God is able to cause all things—good, bad, and otherwise—to work together on behalf of those who love Him and are called according to the purpose He created them for. He is able to take even the things the Liar means for evil—the bad things done to you, even the circumstances over which you had no choice—and use them for your good and to bring further revelation of His love to mankind *through* even the worst hand life could deal you."

"I don't understand," replied Jake.

"You did not need to see me in those pictures until

this moment. Let them be to you a simple confirmation of the fact that what I am telling you is true."

"Okay," said Jake.

"You can either live in darkness or live in light. You can either experience God's love and presence or you can reject it. You can either settle for momentary personal comfort or settle for God's Truth. You can have a life of merely coping or you can have a life lived in abundance in spite of your circumstances. You can live a full life regardless of how short that life may appear in what mankind calls time. With Father God, it matters not the length of the life lived on Earth, but rather that it was lived in relationship with Him.

"Mankind always has a choice in the matter of how life is lived. Although he does not get to choose the things that tempt him nor does he get to choose the storms or circumstance of life through which he must live, mankind *always* has a choice: How he will respond to his temptations and his circumstances. He can either choose to see and respond from God's point of view or from the viewpoint of the Liar. It is *your* choice, Jake. It all depends upon your point of view."

Jake just sat there, rapt with anticipation of all that was being and would be shared—by an angel!

"We've got time so let me show you Father's point of view. Jake, everything you have experienced can either be a weight around your neck that drags you down to self-pity and hopelessness or those same experiences can be cut away, and the very same stones that once hung around your neck can then be used to build memorials that say 'Yes, I went through that, but look what Father God has done!'

"Concerning Old Man Winters. God did not cause that. The Liar did. His only power is that of deception. Old Man Winters was deceived into thinking only sex with a boy could meet his need. You were deceived into thinking giving in to his advances would somehow make you feel wanted, somehow protect your mother from being harmed. Someone get you through. Who do you think protected you from something worse all those years?

"Concerning Happy. The Liar wanted you to feel death to such a degree that you would give up on living and loving. Father used that little puppy to teach you the value of life, the power of a caregiver's love, the passion that now serves you as protector of and provider for Brock and Nadia. For Livy.

"Concerning the public humiliation in the gym. The Liar wanted you to feel complete rejection. Father wanted you to be able to identify with the shame Jesus bore on the cross...the utter shame and nakedness...the scorn...the mocking...the laying down of life... seeing and meeting the needs of others as a means of living a full and fulfilling existence here on Earth. And remember? That's the day you first met Livy. First experienced someone standing in the gap for you. The day you met your soul mate. You always have a choice as to which point of view you will live your life by.

"Concerning your dad's drunkenness, anger, inability to express real love to you, and his inability to properly love your mother: The Liar was about complete annihilation of your lineage. Your collective family destiny for the Kingdom of God. Do you not now have a deep compassion for other men? Were you not instrumental in the way your father was able to turn his own life around? Were you not able to see how hurt your dad had been at the hand of his own father? Would you understand the sweetness of the rain had you never experienced such desert times in your life?

"And do your remember the dreams of your youth? The ones where you were captured and about to be put to death? The ones where, at the last possible moment, your father—the king—would swoop in and rescue you?"

Jake chimed in, "You mean those recurring dreams I had from childhood until I was a married man? The dreams that made me think I was losing my mind all those years?"

"Yes. Those are the ones. How did you feel each morning as you woke up?" asked Michael.

"Well, they woke me up at the same time every morning for years right at the moment I was...rescued..." said Jake, now very solemn.

"That was you?" he asked, looking at Michael.

"Yes, that was me—Father, rather—who wanted you to feel rescued. To feel hope. To keep longing for...Him," replied the angel.

"He is the God of imagination and creativity. He is the God of hope and life. He is the God who has never once—not even for one nanosecond—*ever* left your side.

It is He Who is with you now. I represent Him to you in a form you can comprehend. Jake, He has always been and will always be with you.

"What are you thinking right now, Jake?"

"Wouldn't the better question be 'What are you feeling?' because I feel like I should be losing my mind. But I feel peace," Jake replied.

"Jake, the peace you are experiencing is the right feeling. The Liar has always tried to get you to live by and be defined by the way you feel. Truth is this: Every feeling you have has been born of a thought you have had. Do you remember the statement I made to you a few moments ago?"

"What statement do you mean?" asked Jake.

"I can tell you the very moment that all changed..." said Michael.

"Yes," said Jake.

"Your life, your entire existence, your entire being, was transformed the moment—the split second—you changed your thoughts about Father God. When your thoughts turned from doubt to trust, you went from dark to light. When you changed the way you thought about yourself to thinking about yourself the way He thinks of you, you went from loser to champion, from victim to victor. The moment you changed the way you thought about your dad, you went from 'Poor me' to 'How can I lay down my life for my dad and express to him the love he never got from his own dad?' Jake, as a man thinks, so he is."

The moment Jake went from unbelief to belief in

God, from thinking Jesus was a legend to the realization that he was the remedy for his own sin, he felt so free—like a weight of unbearable magnitude had been lifted from his young shoulders. And he felt that way...now...in this moment...just moments from death. Yet, peace.

"Jake, you have always been loved. You have always had the power to renew and transform your own mind, to change the way you think. You have always had the power to choose your response to any given situation. Always. And you have that power now."

"Life is so short, Michael. My life has been too short. I have not done everything I wanted to do. Haven't gotten to teach my son things. To have tea parties with Nadia. To grow old with Livy. To experience life from what I know now," Jake said, his voice wistful in describing all he was losing.

"Jake, even in such a moment as this, you have that same power. It is not the length of the life that matters; it is the joy experienced along the journey regardless of how it unfolds within the confines of time. God—your Father—is beyond time and you are His son. You have his spiritual DNA flowing in your veins. You are beyond time, Jake. Lay it down while you still can."

18

TO KNOW AND BE KNOWN

> Human beings must be known to be loved; but Divine beings must be loved to be known.
>
> BLAISE PASCAL

> Gratitude unlocks the fullness of life. It turns what we have into enough, and more. It turns denial into acceptance, chaos to order, and confusion to clarity. It can turn a meal into a feast, a house into a home, a stranger into a friend.
>
> MELODY BEATTIE

Acceptance opens a can of worms. If Jake accepted his fate, did that mean that he was giving up? He had battled feeling like a loser for a great portion of his life, but had changed his mind many years ago. Yet here he was, faced with the possibility once again. If he accepted all Michael was saying to him, did that make him a lunatic? He had battled such thoughts through the years as they related to the difference between faith and reality. He had concluded that what was not of faith was not reality. If he accepted Michael's words concerning the concept of time, did that change the fact that he was going to die? In that moment, he began to realize that he had lived a long life in a short time. The question became, "Have I lived my life well?"

Although the plane was soon to crash, Jake became strangely indifferent to the passing of time. His thoughts of fighting the plunge turned into going with the flow. He had learned a long time ago that if he could not change his circumstances, he could change the way he thought about them. If he was going to die, death would not win. By faith in Christ he was convinced that though his body would soon experience death, his spirit —the very core of his identity—would certainly live on. And then he thought the most absurd of all thoughts: "I might as well enjoy the ride."

Michael broke into his awareness at that very moment. "Yes, Jake. Enjoy the ride."

Jake was suddenly back at the altar, face to face with his bride, Livy. As he looked into her eyes, he saw into eternity. At that moment he had imagined living out the rest of his days with her. Making babies with her. Raising those children with her. Growing old together. Experiencing life with her.

Life. He remembered how he felt on their wedding day. How he was finally getting a hold on this thing called life. Feeling as if he finally had a semblance of a clue as to how things really worked. And, in a sense, he had. From the moment their love was consummated on their wedding night, he came to the understanding why waiting had been so necessary. His willingness to wait to make love to his bride had communicated value and worth to her and to all those whose lives would intersect with his. His college acquaintances all teased him about Livy's virginity and his vow to remain pure until the wedding night. Some had mocked him. Others simply thought him weirdly old-fashioned, never being able to see the lack of guilt and shame such a commitment meant to the healing of his own soul.

Waiting. Waiting had built in him, or released in him, what had been planted in his heart the moment he had placed his faith in Jesus: A deep awareness of the value of others. Those who before faith would have intimidated him now made him aware of the depravity of their own deep needs for love and acceptance and affirmation and approval. He had learned from Max Jones that everyone has the same basic need: to know and to be known. This truth had set him free when placed within the parameters of the Divine order of things. He had come to view life—the universe itself—from a grand perspective. He realized that life lived outside those parameters was not freedom at all. He understood that the very boundaries the world called stifling and puritanical were actually the road signs to real relationship with God. The way he had come to view his own life was rather simple. Being familiar with the operating system of his laptop, he knew that for the computer to operate at prime power—in freedom—it needed to work within the parameters of the operation system. When that operating system acquired a bug or when he tried to use it for something never intended for its use, he found glitches, frustration, chaos and bondage! He had found life lived apart from God's order to be the same. As he had learned to change his thoughts and perspectives from self-centered to Christ-centered, the glitches and frustration and chaos and bondage gave way to freedom.

Jake suddenly recognized, mid free-fall, that he felt free because he *was* free! He had, indeed, experienced the sexual abuse, the emotional abuse, the unfairness of life, but none of those things—not one of them—defined who he was. As the plane whistled at more than 500 miles per hour, carrying Jake and all those other souls toward eternity, he leaned back in his seat and smiled.

He began to sing an old song he had heard in church one day as He and Livy worshiped Jesus together amidst hundreds of others.

For all that You've done, I will thank You
For all that You're going to do
For all that You've promised and all that You are
Is all that has carried me through
Jesus, I thank You
And I thank You! Thank You, Lord!
And I thank You! Thank You, Lord!

Thank You for loving and setting me free!
Thank You for giving Your life just for me! How I thank You!
Jesus, I thank You!
Gratefully thank You!
Thank You

"Do you know that song, Michael?" asked Jake

"Yes, of course I know it," replied the messenger.

"Sing with me," said Jake, innocently and sincerely.

"I cannot sing that song, Jake," said Michael.

"Do angels not sing?" asked Jake

"Of course, we sing but we cannot sing that which we have not experienced," explained Michael

"I do not understand," replied Jake.

"The song you sing is a song of the redeemed. Those whom Jesus the Christ shed His redeeming blood to purchase. You have been redeemed. I have not because I have never sinned. I will never be able to understand the joy, the sheer awareness of God's love and forgiveness, His sweet mercy, and His pure and perfect love like you, Jake. That song is yours to sing."

Right then, Jake felt an awareness. A presence. A specialness. A reverence. An awe. A majesty. And it took his breath away even as oxygen flowed out of the mask covering his face. He had experienced a similar feeling before, a feeling of presence with Him, that day he had given his heart to Jesus. That day he said, "I do" to Livy. The day Brock was born. The day Nadia had graced his life. The day he had realized he was no one's victim. The day he realized he was a victor over all his past. The moment he realized God loved him right where he was and loved him enough to not leave him there.

And then it clicked. God was there. God was with Him. Time stood still and all Jake could do was express unabashed gratitude for things the world would have thought foolish.

He thanked God for Old Man Winters. Thanked Him for taking the guilt and shame and wound upon wound and replacing them with forgiveness and naked and unashamed relationship with his Maker and healing the deepest wounds he thought no one would ever be able to reach.

He thanked God for the day he had been left naked and afraid in the gym. He thanked the Presence for even the humiliation he had experienced that day. Thanked Him for the rescue. For the sweetness of Livy's innocent smile piercing the hurt and shame.

He thanked God for his dad's anger. For all the beatings. For every time his face had been slapped. For the day his mom and grandma had to pull Owen off of him. Thanked Him for the depth of God's cleansing surpassing the depths of despair to which he had sunk during such depravity at the hands of his own flesh and blood.

"Michael, do you feel that?" asked Jake.

Michael did not respond. He was down on his knees, hands covering his face, and something within Jake told him Michael not only felt but also was bowing in sheer reverence to the presence of God.

Not wanting to disturb Michael's awareness of the Creator of the universe, Jake simply asked out loud, "How is gratitude for something evil and terrible even possible? Why is it so...freeing?"

At that very moment, the entire plane shuddered and shook. The air was filled with the sound of the most tremendous thunder. Lightning ricocheted through the entire cabin, yet nothing seemed to be consumed, shattered or burned.

And then, stillness.

The sound of the plane was no more. The sound of crying babies and screaming adults was no more. The sound of a jet careening and screaming through the wind was no more. Suspended in midair, suspended in time, the thunder became a whisper as a Voice spoke.

"To not be able to give thanks in and for any situation is to misunderstand the mystery of life. Life, to be lived in abundance despite the circumstance, requires both giving and receiving. To not forgive is to hold one's own heart captive to a wound. For a wound to be healed, it must be opened and cleansed. To not forgive hinders the very thing desired. Healing. Comfort. Cleansing. Wholeness.

"Relationship is everything. To not see life from My point of view is to build a dam that prevents the very thing desired. The life that flows down from the surrounding hills and into and through the Sea of Galilee—a living sea, full of life and living things—is the same life that flows in the Jordan River. The same life that flows through the River Jordan is the very same life that flows into the Dead Sea, yet the Dead Sea is dead. Why, Jake, is it dead though it receives the same life?"

Jake did not hesitate. "It has no life because it does not give. It only receives. Real life—truly living—requires both giving and receiving. Life that is not laid down is not truly lived. Life that does not receive life is not fully lived. Life that is not lived according to the order of the One Who made it is not lived in abundance...is not really living."

"Do you wish to live, Jake?" asked the Voice. "Are you hungry?"

19

DEATH

The boundaries which divide Life from Death are at best shadowy and vague. Who shall say where the one ends, and where the other begins?

EDGAR ALLAN POE

The fear of death follows from the fear of life. A man who lives fully is prepared to die at any time.

MARK TWAIN

"Am I hungry?" asked Jake.

"Even now, I have given you something you have dreamed of," said the Voice.

Looking down, Jake saw steam rising from his butter-soaked baked potato and smelled the aroma emanating from his much-anticipated steak.

"But...Sir...how can I eat now? I'll—we'll all be—dead in a matter of seconds."

"Whether you live or whether you die, who do you belong to, Jake? Whether you live or die, where will you be? Why do you worry about what any one of these other people think or compare yourself to them in any way? They are each being ministered to just as you are. Concern yourself with your own soul right now, son, and live."

"Live." And suddenly Jake's memories found Livy and saw her "life after Jake." He saw her sadness and felt thankful that she had gone through the process of grief and found the healing aspects of mourning. In that moment of personal grief at the thought of his short life on Earth, Jake understood the difference between grief and mourning. Grief is the pain of loss. Mourning is the outward expression of that grief, the expression of that pain. He saw Livy as she mourned his loss and got the pain out of her soul and onto the broad and able and massive shoulders of the Lord. And as he mourned for his own loss, he gave that loss to the Voice and received comfort like he had never known. Comfort better than a child experiences on a stormy night when they find shelter beneath the covers, nestled between their parents. He felt clean. Safe. And he knew Livy would be fine. That she would always honor his memory and long for the day she would see him again.

"Daddy! Daddy! Do it again! Throw me high! Throw me up to the sky, daddy! Again!" said little Brock. In that moment of suspended time, Jake relived every moment he had spent with his son. So many times he had thrown his son into the air, giving Brock the sensation of flying. The look of glee and trust shining from his face like a thousand suns. He saw Brock in the days to come "after dad went to be with Jesus." He heard Livy telling their son to remember what daddy would say. She told Brock how proud his dad would be of the way he chose to respond to those who said unkind things. How proud his dad would be at the way he valued life. How proud he would be at the way he treated those less fortunate than himself. And Jake saw his grandsons. He saw Brock throwing them into the air as he declared, "My daddy used to do the same thing with me! Fly, boys! Fly!"

As tears streamed down his face, Jake's thoughts turned toward his precious little girl. The girl he never got to have tea parties with. The girl who never got to put her dad's hair in pony tails and never got to do his nails. He saw another man—Livy's older brother, Jim—walking Nadia down the aisle. He heard his brother-in-law whisper into her ear, "Your dad is looking down on you right now, sweetheart."

He heard her say, "I know, uncle Jim. I feel him." As she danced with her new husband, he listened in as she told him, "My dad loved my mom this way. Thank you for waiting for me. Thank you for fighting for my virtue. Thank you for laying down your life for me like my daddy did." And he saw her as she turned her head toward him and gave him a little glance toward heaven that only a dad and a daughter could give one another and said, "I love you, daddy."

In the span of eternity contained in a nanosecond, he was able to see the times and loves of his children from the vantage point of the Creator. He heard Brock crying in the night for daddy. He heard the cries of his little girl growing up without her daddy, wishing she could have known him. He heard the cries of his children as they—when the time had been right—cried out to Daddy God and found their eternal needs met in a moment's time.

Daddy. A word. A name that had once caused so much pain for Jake had become a name synonymous with joy, peace, safety and love. And then Jake felt a presence next to him. But it was not the presence of the Voice he felt. Not the presence of Michael. He turned to see a face he had not seen since that day he had said goodbye at his father's funeral. "Dad...how... did you get here?" Jake asked as their eyes met.

"I am here at His Word, son," said Owen.

"But...is this...real? Are you really here?" queried Jake.

"I am as real as it gets, son," replied Owen.

"But why now?" Jake mustered.

"I'm here to tell you it's all going to be okay. You have nothing to fear. I'm here, son. Daddy's here."

As suddenly as a bolt of lightning striking the ground, Jake began pouring out his heart to his dad.

"Dad, I am so sorry I never got to say goodbye. By

the time they called me to the hospital, you had already drifted into a coma, and then you were just...gone."

"I heard you, son. Heard every word." "What do you mean?" asked Jake. "There—at the side of my bed—I heard it all. Heard you ask me to forgive you. Heard you say you had forgiven me. Heard you say how much you had wanted to say. Heard you say it all. Heard you say goodbye. Heard you say... how much you loved me."

Jake sat in stunned silence, his mind reeling at all that had transpired in the last sixty seconds since he had just been served his meal. Since the plane had begun to fall from the sky. Still reeling from the immense awareness of the very presence of God and eternity he was trying to fathom with his frail and finite human brain. And now his dad was sitting right next to him!

"Son, in earthly time, you do not have much time. So...live."

Jake wondered why everyone was telling him to live when death was so near!

"Son," interrupted Owen, "It's okay. Remember how you told me there in my hospital bed that it was 'okay to let go?'"

Jake nodded.

"Son, it's okay to let go and live."

Turning to look his dad square in the eye—something he had never really experienced in their relationship—Jake asked, "Does it hurt?"

"Dying is fairly easy, son. And you will feel no pain

as the plane meets the ground. Your brain will not have time to even comprehend it, so why be afraid? It's going to be okay."

"Can you stay with me, dad?"

"No, son. I cannot walk this road with you, but you will not be alone. Michael will walk through with you and Father will carry you through."

And as suddenly as he had appeared, Owen Owens was gone and Michael was sitting next to Jake once again. Reaching out to touch Jake, Michael said, "I know you have been given much in the span of these few seconds of earthly time, but what you have experienced will serve you well in the days to come."

"How can that be when I am about to die?" asked Jake.

"Jake, human life, at best, is a vapor in the span of eternity. The short life. Every life is short when seen from the vantage point of eternity. The real question is how you will live the life you've been given regardless of the time spent living it.

"Michael, what is heaven like?" asked Jake, seeming to have finally succumbed to the thought of impending doom.

"Everything you call good on Earth is only expanded and intensified and purified in the eternal home. Mountain vistas can be experienced without aid of oxygen tanks. Cold will be experienced without fear of frostbite. Water can be explored without the need of breathing apparatus or goggles. Flight can be experienced without wings. Relationship is experienced more fully than your present human mind can even comprehend. In that place, the lion lays down with the lamb. The wolf shares the same realm as the dove. Fear is nonexistent. Tears will cease. Sorrow and suffering and pain and death are no more. And He—the Presence, the Voice, the Father, The Spirit, the Son, the Savior Who is Redeemer, Jesus —is the Light of the universe. In Him everything exists and moves and has its being. You will see...so...live, Jake. Live."

Live. That word again. Jake had once been confused but now he began to see. Life is meant to be lived abundantly. Regardless of how long. In spite of the failures. In spite of the circumstances. In spite of physical or emotional or mental frailties. It is best lived when lived according to the Order ordained from the Creator. Meant to be lived even when dying.

Such thoughts reduced Jake to complete peace. Without saying another word to Michael, he leaned back in his seat and pushed the button, bringing his seat to the upright and locked position.

Taking his fork in his right hand and the sharp steak knife in his left, Jake closed his eyes and took in the moment. As the sweet smell of butter mixed with the intense smell of freshly oak-grilled steak filled his senses, Jake took a bite of potato. Like it was the first time he had ever tasted such savory goodness, he simply muttered, "Mmmm...mmmm...mmmm."

Cutting into the perfectly cooked piece of meat, he cut a man-sized piece and dipped it into the butter that had melted like sweet lava onto the plate from the heat of the potato. Chewing as if it was the last meal of a dying man, he savored every flavor. Jake ate his steak, determined that, no matter how long or short his life, he would live.

He would live well.

JOIN ME ON PATREON

Would you like to receive exclusive music, updates, teaching, and new releases?

Visit www.patreon.com/dennisjernigan to learn how you can get all this and more.

DON'T MISS A THING

Would you like to receive email newsletters from me?

You'll receive periodic news, updates, offers, and prayer requests. There's no obligation and I'll never spam you. Don't miss out on another update!

Visit dennisjernigan.com/newsletter to sign up.

DID YOU ENJOY THIS BOOK?

Did you enjoy this book? You can make a big difference by leaving a review.

Reviews are one of the most important ways authors reach new readers. I don't have the funds to reach new people through advertising, but I have something more valuable, a group of individuals who support and believe in my ministry.

If you enjoyed this book, would you consider leaving an honest review? It doesn't need to be long. Your review will help other readers find this book.

To leave a review, simply visit your preferred ebook vendor and leave a review for The Short Life.

ALSO BY DENNIS JERNIGAN

The Chronicles of Bren

A fantasy adventure series for young adults

Captured

Sacrifice

Generations

The Bairns of Bren

A fantasy adventure series for young readers

Hide and Seek

The Light Eater

Short Stories for Children

The Incredible Growing Basketball Goal

Daddy's Song

The Christmas Dream

Fiction for Adults

A Thread of Hope

The Short Life

Non-fiction

Sing Over Me: An Autobiography

Renewing Your Mind: Identity and the Matter of Choice

Music

Celebrate Living

First Love

The Worshiper's Collection, Volume 3

DVD

Sing Over Me: The Dennis Jernigan Documentary

Many other recordings, books, and resources are available at www.dennisjernigan.com.

WHO IS DENNIS JERNIGAN?

Dennis Jernigan is a Kingdom Seeker. On November 7, 1981 he was given a brand new identity and walked out of his old homosexual identity and into the Kingdom of God. He began to seek Jesus—the King—and not a ministry, yet ministry has flowed out of his life in world-reaching ways. His songs are sung in tens of thousands of churches around the world each and every week. His story is read and heard and recounted to thousands each month via YouTube, Facebook, dennisjernigan.com, and his many speaking and concert engagements.

Through the years, Dennis has been privileged to work with the likes of Dr. James Dobson, Steve Farrar, Anne Graham Lotz, James Robison, Beth Moore, Max Lucado, and Andy Comiskey and has recorded with

Annie Herring, Matthew Ward, Alvin Slaughter, Rebecca St. James, Travis Cottrell, Charlie Hall, Natalie Grant, Ron Kenoly, Christie Nockels, First Call, and Twila Paris.

Dennis Jernigan's mission statement can be boiled down to this:

> The Spirit of the Lord is upon me, because he anointed me to preach the gospel to the poor. He has sent me to proclaim release to the captives, and recovery of sight to the blind, to set free those who are oppressed, to proclaim the favorable year of the Lord.
>
> LUKE 4:18-19

Dennis lives with his wife, Melinda, in Muskogee, OK, where they raised their nine children. They are now welcoming many grandchildren.

To book Dennis Jernigan for ministry, call (1)-918-781-1200 or simply email us at mail@dennisjernigan.com.

For more information:
www.dennisjernigan.com
mail@dennisjernigan.com
patron.com/dennisjernigan

facebook.com/official.dennisjernigan
youtube.com/dennisjernigan
amazon.com/author/dennisjernigan
twitter.com/dennisjernigan
instagram.com/dennisjernigan

www.ingramcontent.com/pod-product-compliance
Lightning Source LLC
Chambersburg PA
CBHW070457170726
48291CB00008B/2545
9781948772099